DI036253

<u>Are You On Our Email List?</u>

<u>Sign up on our website</u>

<u>www.thecartelpublications.com</u>

<u>Or text the word:</u>

<u>Cartelbooks to 22828</u>

<u>For prizes, contests, etc.</u>

CHECK OUT OTHER TITLES BY THE CARTEL PUBLICATIONS

SHYT LIST 1: BE CAREFUL WHO YOU CROSS

SHYT LIST 2: LOOSE CANNON

SHYT LIST 3: AND A CHILD SHALL LEAVE THEM

SHYT LIST 4: CHILDREN OF THE WRONGED

SHYT LIST 5: SMOKIN' CRAZIES THE FINALE'

PITBULLS IN A SKIRT 1

PITBULLS IN A SKIRT 2

PITBULLS IN A SKIRT 3: THE RISE OF LIL C

PITBULLS IN A SKIRT 4: KILLER KLAN

PITBULLS IN A SKIRT 5: THE FALL FROM GRACE

POISON 1

POISON 2

VICTORIA'S SECRET

HELL RAZOR HONEYS 1

HELL RAZOR HONEYS 2

BLACK AND UGLY

BLACK AND UGLY AS EVER

MISS WAYNE & THE QUEENS OF DC

BLACK AND THE UGLIEST

A HUSTLER'S SON

A HUSTLER'S SON 2

THE FACE THAT LAUNCHED A THOUSAND BULLETS

YEAR OF THE CRACKMOM

THE UNUSUAL SUSPECTS

LA FAMILIA DIVIDED

RAUNCHY

RAUNCHY 2: MAD'S LOVE

RAUNCHY 3: JAYDEN'S PASSION

MAD MAXXX: CHILDREN OF THE CATACOMBS (EXTRA RAUNCHY)

KALI: RAUNCHY RELIVED: THE MILLER FAMILY

REVERSED

QUITA'S DAYSCARE CENTER

QUITA'S DAYSCARE CENTER 2

DEAD HEADS

DRUNK & HOT GIRLS

PRETTY KINGS

PRETTY KINGS 2: SCARLETT'S FEVER

By KIM MEDINA   5

GAY FOR MY BAE

THE END. HOW TO WRITE A BESTSELLING NOVEL IN 30 DAYS

WWW.THECARTELPUBLICATIONS.COM

THE HOUSE THAT CRACK

BUILT 4:

REGGIE & AMINA

By

KIM MEDINA

Copyright © 2018 by The Cartel Publications. All
rights reserved.
No part of this book may be reproduced in any
form without permission
from the author, except by reviewer who may quote
passages
to be printed in a newspaper or magazine.

PUBLISHER'S NOTE:
This book is a work of fiction. Names, characters,
businesses,
Organizations, places, events and incidents are the
product of the
Author's imagination or are used fictionally. Any
resemblance of
Actual persons, living or dead, events, or locales
are entirely coincidental.

Library of Congress Control Number: 2018953135

ISBN 10: 1948373084

ISBN 13: 978-1948373081

Cover Design: Bookslutgirl.com

www.thecartelpublications.com
First Edition
Printed in the United States of America

What's Up Fam,

I hope and pray that you all have had a wonderful and blessed summer. Although it's already August, meaning summer is coming to an end, I'm boosted about the great news and new releases The Cartel Publications has coming up.

One in particular, the novel in your hands, "The House That Crack Built 4: Reggie & Amina". I could not wait to get a hold of this one, especially after the way Kim left part 3. I was pressed to find out what happens next and I must say, this book satisfied all my nosey needs. I know you gonna enjoy it as much as I did.

With that being said, keeping in line with tradition, we want to give respect to a vet or new trailblazer paving the way. In this novel, we would like to recognize:

LENA WAITHE

Lena Waithe is an American screenwriter and producer. She's also the FIRST African American woman to win an Emmy for Outstanding writing for a Comedy series for her contribution on, *Master of None*, the "Thanksgiving" episode. She is also the writer and creator of Showtime's series, "The Chi". We are very proud of Lena and her accomplishments. Make sure you check out her work!

Aight, no more delay, get to it. I'll catch you in the next book.

Be Easy!

Charisse "C. Wash" Washington
Vice President
The Cartel Publications
www.thecartelpublications.com
www.facebook.com/publishercwash
Instagram: publishercwash
www.twitter.com/cartelbooks
www.facebook.com/cartelpublications
Follow us on Instagram: Cartelpublications
#CartelPublications
#UrbanFiction

#PrayForCeCe

#PrayForJuneMiller

#LenaWaithe

CARTEL URBAN CINEMA'S WEB SERIES

BMORE CHICKS

@ Pink Crystal Inn

NOW AVAILABLE:

Via

YOUTUBE

And

DVD

(Season 2 Coming Soon)

www.youtube.com/user/tstyles74

www.cartelurbancinema.com

www.thecartelpublications.com

#TheHouseThatCrackBuilt4

PROLOGUE

*E*veryone had a glass of liquor in hand to celebrate Tamika's birthday. And although she wore a smile on her face the only thing on her mind was the two seats to the left and right of her that were empty. Even with thirteen people present the absence of Amina and Reggie stood out to Tamika like a cracked windowpane. The only one there that understood what she was going through was Russo. Russo softly grabbed her hand.

"Don't," he said.

She snatched away.

After three minutes she walked outside and found them out back by the dumpsters. Amina was crying and Reggie was consoling her. Easing closer, but away from their sight, she could hear it all.

"I know it hurts but you gotta chill out," Reggie said.

"Chill out?" Amina yelled. *"It's easy for you to say. You have both of us."*

"Don't say that."

"It's true."

"So you gonna fake like you and Russo not together?"

"Reggie, Russo barely stays at the house and he hasn't touched me in months."

"He better not."

"You see what I'm saying?" Amina yelled pulling away from him. *"You don't want me fucking my own husband but you can still sleep with Tamika?"*

"Man, Tamika's drive is high and all I do is finger her and eat her out." He lied. *"My dick belongs to you."*

Amina took a deep breath." I can't do this forever. I want you to myself."

"Then stop acting up every time we all together. I gotta give Tamika some attention sometimes especially on her birthday. But when I can, the moment I can, I'm leaving her for you. Aight?"

Tamika sobbed quietly to herself.

If he thought leaving her would be easy he was in for a rude awakening. One that resembled hell.

CHAPTER ONE

TAMIKA

I was helping Russo push weights in the back of our house to strengthen his legs. The doctor said Russo would never walk again and now almost a year later he was working on running after mastering walking. I guess when you put your mind to it you can prove everybody wrong.

"I'm so proud of you," I said giving him a towel. "You're my inspiration."

He wiped his face. "Go ahead with that shit."

"I'm serious, Russo." I shoved his arm. "You are stronger than ever. Even after everything you've been through."

"Nah." He tossed the towel on his bench. "I ain't at a hundred yet but it's a start." He paused and looked me in the eyes and I could tell he was about to go deep. "I just wanna thank you for always being there for me. And for helping me walk again."

"Now listen at you," I said grabbing my purse and car keys off the chair. "You buttering me up hard. I feel like you about to ask me for something." I laughed.

"I'm dead ass for real," he said. "I know it's been hard watching me like this and—"

"My sister and husband fall deeper in love." I paused. "Because if you about to say that you're right."

He nodded. "Yeah." He took a deep breath. "But we'll rap about that later. Where you about to go?"

"To get my hair done."

"Hold off right quick."

My eyes widened. "Why?"

"Hey, man, you 'aight?" Reggie asked coming around the side of the house. "I got your text."

"Yeah, I'm good." Russo said. "Just wanted to rap to you about something."

"Russo, are you okay?" Amina asked coming out the back door.

I tried not to glare at them both but it was hard. Russo and I knew they were together and yet they tried to fake like that wasn't the case.

Russo cleared his throat. "Yeah things are fine. But, uh, I'm moving out."

My heart thumped.

Russo was my partner in this house. He was the only reason that I didn't confront them on many occasions. But if I'm being fair, his reason was understandable I guess. He was worried that my niece, his daughter, would be surrounded by anger in a broken home. That was the understanding so what changed now?

"Why you moving?" Reggie frowned, his voice heavy with guilt whether he knew it or not.

"Need more space."

"I understand," Amina said.

"I bet you do." Russo responded.

"No, I'm serious. You need more space for your workout equipment and stuff."

Silence.

Russo glared at her and I could tell he was feeling what I was thinking. That she was way too excited for a woman who just heard that her husband was leaving.

"I mean, I want you comfortable, Russo," Amina added.

"Yeah, well I already set up a spot," Russo continued. "I'll be out by Saturday."

When Russo walked away I followed. I could tell his feelings were hurt by her reaction but he'd never let me know. "What are you doing?" I asked him.

"It's time to move on, Tamika. I want the best for my daughter but I'm still a street nigga. I mean, you know how hard it was for me not to kill that dude?" He said as we stood in the front yard. "He's still alive because I know you still love him and my daughter is everything to me."

Tears rolled down my cheek and he wiped them away before pulling me into a big hug. Something that made me feel better every time he had done it throughout the months.

"Come with me, Tamika." He said as he looked into my eyes. "I got plenty of space for you."

"But, I mean..."

"You can't stay here and watch this shit," he said. "They wanna be together then fuck 'em. You shouldn't have to kill yourself with hurt while it happens."

By KIM MEDINA   21

"I'm not leaving until I make both of them pay for what they did to you and me. And since I'm speaking my mind, I'm kinda fucked up with you for not sticking by my side and helping me." I stormed toward my car and pulled off.

CHAPTER TWO

AMINA

I was so happy about Russo leaving that I couldn't stop from moving excitedly in place. And then I saw Reggie's face. We were still in the backyard and I walked over toward him.

"What's wrong with you?" I said smiling. "With Russo leaving the only thing we have to work on is Tamika. This is what we wanted," I grinned. "Be happy."

"That shit ain't weird to you?"

"What you mean?"

He frowned. "Mina, your husband just said he bouncing. Don't you give a fuck a little?"

"No, I don't."

He pulled away from me. "You starting to scare me. I mean, you didn't even ask why. What if they know we fuckin'?"

"Reggie, you must've thought I was playing when I said I was done with Russo. Now you can tell I'm serious."

He frowned at me and walked around the front of the house. I walked inside and Tamika was in the kitchen. She was so green and gullible that it was pathetic. Here I was fucking her husband right under her nose and she could care less.

"Are you and Russo okay?" She asked.

"Yeah, why you say that?" I opened the cabinet and grabbed a yellow cup.

"He said he was leaving and you acted like you didn't care. I know ya'll had problems in the past but—"

"You reading into things wrong." I paused. "I love my husband but I can't force—"

"Are you okay, Amina?" She asked. "For real?"

I slammed the cup on the counter. "You know what, stay the fuck out my business before you get your feelings hurt."

"Amina, I'm sorry if you thought I was intruding."

"It ain't about being sorry." I stepped closer. "It's about you always finding a reason to be concerned with my life. What you need to do is worry about your own husband and what's going on with him."

"What that mean?"

I walked upstairs.

I know some may think its wrong that I'm fucking Reggie on the side but it's more than just sex with us. I love him because I know no matter what, that he gets me and has my back. Maybe his dysfunction in life matches mine and that's why we mesh so well together.

Who knows.

All I can say is that I'll never let him go.

When my cell phone rang on my bed I quickly grabbed it, hoping it was Reggie asking me to meet him around the corner so I could suck him off in the car. We fight a lot but for the most part we always come back together.

When I answered my phone I was irritated when I heard my cousin April's voice. I rolled my eyes and said, "What?"

"Don't sound all crazy," She said. "And why you ain't been answering the phone when I hit you? I hardly hear from you these days unless you need a sitter. Which brings me to my next question. You know I'm headed to the gym. Why you ain't pick up your daughter?"

"Girl, I was busy but you can drop Naverly off if she's all that trouble. You ain't got to keep nothing that's mine because she's gonna be alright."

"Don't act like I don't be getting my little cousin, Amina. I just have some running around to do and my husband is taking me out later tonight."

"I said bring her back!" I yelled. "Fuck you want me to say now? I'm here and if I'm not Tamika got her."

I was about to hang up when she said, "Wait, though. I still miss you, Amina. We haven't talked in like forever." She paused. "What's been going on in your world?"

I knew this bitch was reaching and I wasn't going to give her the satisfaction. Plus I was cautious of anybody asking a bunch of questions and April was famous for it. Specifically when it came to who I was fucking.

Back in the day I would've told my cousin I was dealing with Reggie but I didn't trust her after she slept with my boyfriend in high school. Plus she acted like she was better than everybody and probably wouldn't understand.

Don't get me wrong. I know my cousin changed and even got married last month but I still was weary of her. Reggie made me lose reason sometimes and I couldn't explain the fear I had of losing him. The last thing I wanted was some negative ass opinions from people who meant nothing to me.

Maybe it was the sex or maybe it was the way he held me in his arms so tight. Whatever it was I couldn't be sure. All I knew was he was mine and our lives were private.

"Maybe we can talk later," I said grabbing my robe off the door. "I'm about to jump in the shower."

"Okay. I just wanted you to know I'm here and you don't have to go through your struggles alone."

I hung up on her.

Fake ass.

It was time to get fresh, douche and prepare dinner. Because my plan was to fuck the hair off Reggie's back tonight.

It's time to celebrate!

CHAPTER THREE

REGGIE

The red head sucking my dick in my car was pretty good and just what I needed.

I was parked behind the gym because I didn't want to risk her changing her mind about topping me off. It started with me helping her lift weights and the next minute we were here.

She talked so much shit over the months that I wanted her to make good on the promise. She did just that. When she was done she wiped the corners of her mouth with her fingertips and smiled at me.

"That was quick," she said. "I was hoping I could taste you longer."

"You shouldn't be so good."

She smiled. "Your dick was sweet."

She was saying a lot right now when for real all I wanted was for her to get gone. "Thanks." I pinched her face. "But look, I gotta get back inside and finish my set. We gonna talk about me taking care of you later."

She winked again, got out and walked back inside without another word. Yep, she was used to playing the thot.

When she was gone I leaned back and sighed. If there was anything I wanted to say about myself it was this...I needed to get my sex drive under control but I didn't know where to begin. I even started seeing another psychiatrist after changing them five times because I fucked four of 'em.

To get that under control, this time I hired a dude but since I just finished fucking a girl I worked out with in the gym, I can honestly say he's not working.

I feared if I couldn't pull myself away from my habit that it was gonna mean my life.

When my phone rang I answered it.

"Come home, Reggie," Amina said. "Please."

"I'm at the gym."

"I know but I miss you."

"You know how I am about my body," I said. "You should be in here too."

"What that supposed to mean?"

"I just told you, Amina."

"So it's my fault I can't go to the gym and got a little thick because I—"

"Let me call you back."

When I hung up on her I saw her cousin April walking toward the gym. I rushed up to her after getting out the car and was able to catch her before she walked into the locker room.

"Aye, girl," I said.

She turned around, smiled and hugged me. "Hey! I didn't know you worked out here."

"It's the closest gym to the crib."

She nodded. "Well you look good. Getting all ripped up and shit."

"Thanks," I took her comment to mean she wanted to fuck me but I had to be careful. One wrong move and I could make things worse on the home front. Something I didn't need right now. I had a wife and a girlfriend and I didn't need another relationship.

Even though I will say this, Tamika gave me no grief lately at home. She didn't ask me where I was going or when I was getting back. She seemed to be more interested in making me happy than anything else and the guilt weighed on me but wasn't heavy enough to stop doing my thing.

To be honest I was surprised she was so green when it came to me but also relieved. I didn't want to throw it up in Amina's face that my wife was easy going but I definitely thought about it, especially because she was the exact opposite lately.

"But let me get in this locker room so I can get on this treadmill. This body ain't gonna work itself," she laughed.

It's sure not. I thought.

"I'll see you soon," she said.

"You do that," I said rubbing my hands together as I watched her walk inside.

When I felt myself doing too much I asked myself what's wrong with me? Why I gotta be so foul? So when she was gone I dug into my pocket and made a call. "I need to see you."

"Are you safe?" My psychiatrist asked.

"For now. But if I don't get an appointment I'm gonna make a huge mistake."

"Be here in an hour."

CHAPTER FOUR

TAMIKA

"**I** know what you saying, Russo." I said as I sat at the table in his kitchen. He had just purchased an amazing penthouse apartment in downtown DC after selling his house in Maryland.

The government had to give him back his property after he obtained fake documents saying he invested in stocks, which could account for how he was able to buy the house.

"But I can't let it go," I pouted. "They having their way and—"

"You letting them win." He paused to sign a document from one of the many movers entering and leaving his place. They were bringing in furniture.

"Well, I guess they gonna win then." I paused. "I mean I'm not like you."

"Meaning?"

"I'm not over him."

He looked away from me and glared.

What did that mean?

"I get that, Tamika, but you gonna have to get over him soon. I mean, you saw them together yourself. Why would you want a man like that?"

"I need money," I said out of the blue. I didn't wanna hear him say they wanted each other. What I wanted was revenge.

"Money?"

"Russo, I know you got it."

"That's not the question." He paused. "I wanna know what you want it for?"

"My plan."

He sat down. "More explanation."

"I know both of them. I know what they want and what makes them move."

"Tamika, stop this shit."

"Are you gonna give it to me or not?"

He ran his hand down his face. "How much?"

"Twenty grand."

He smiled and shook his head. "Wow, you really going all out aren't you?"

"If that's what you wanna call it."

He sighed. "I don't know 'bout this."

I sat back because he was blowing me. Ever since our neighbor, Mrs. Connelly got into his head he changed. Seemed softer than he was before she entered the picture and I hated that part.

Or maybe it was because of what his cousin did by kidnapping him. After he got better he got his cousin killed and it was like all of his problems were over.

But what about me?

I have been experiencing the worst pain any woman could imagine. I had to endure my sister and husband fall in love while I sat back and watched.

Part of me felt like I was doing it because of what Russo said about wanting my niece to have a safe and calm environment since so much seemed to be going on.

But, I knew what it was really about. If I blew up their spot and he chose her I was afraid I'd go back to drugs due to devastation.

Nah, I wanted to make sure things went my way.

"I'm asking for your help, Russo. You can give me the money or not. But both if them deserve to pay. Please."

CHAPTER FIVE

REGGIE

"She's my wife's cousin." I folded my arms over my chest as I sat across from my psychiatrist who was sitting in a large recliner.

"Okay, do you think she's interested?"

"Don't know."

He nodded and I regretted coming that quickly. Not only because I was wearing white and black shorts since I just came from the gym but also because I didn't know if this shit would even help me.

"So why do you want to pursue her?"

"I'm a man and I'm black." I adjusted in my seat. "You know how we are. We want what we want."

He smiled. "I'm a black man and I don't have a desire to be with more women then I can handle."

I frowned.

"It doesn't make me better and I'm certainly not pointing the finger, Reggie. I'm just—"

"What are you saying then?"

He sighed. "Do you recall your very first sexual experience?"

I smiled. "Yep."

He leaned forward and grinned. "You seem confident."

"It's because I was."

"Tell me more."

I wiped my hand down my face. "Let's just say my girl wasn't prepared. But I knew how to make her feel."

"Wow, for your first girl?"

"Yep."

"How old were you?"

"Eleven or twelve I think."

His smile disappeared. "And how were you, um, how were you so experienced at such a young age?"

"I can't remember."

"You can't remember or you don't want to tell me?"

"You think I would lie?" I frowned.

Silence.

I readjusted in my chair and gripped myself. "I uh..."

"Reggie, do you need to go to the bathroom?"

"Why?"

He looked in my lap at my hand, which was covering my dick. "I saw you, you know."

I removed my hand off myself and crossed my arms over my chest. "Sorry."

"I don't want you to be sorry. I'm here to help you work through things and it's obvious that whenever you're uncomfortable you look for sexual gratification."

I nodded. "All my life I, I used sex as a way to...I mean..."

"I don't want you pushing yourself too hard, Reggie. When the real meaning of you using sex as a crutch is revealed we'll know. Take your time and make sure you don't put yourself under excess pressure."

"You think I'm crazy but I'm not," I said. "I really be trying to control myself but I can't. I just—" I got up and left the office.

You know what, fuck this nigga.

TAMIKA

I had been up all night devising my plan after Russo gave me the money. It took me awhile but in the end I created the perfect situation to ruin their perfect little world.

After being in my room on the phone all day I was officially prepared for part one. Reggie was downstairs playing video games and Amina was at an afternoon doctors appointment with Naverly and Russo was with her.

I walked down the stairs and sat next to Reggie. He looked at me and smiled before focusing back on the game. Fuck he have to smile about? He was ruining my world.

"I'm hungry."

He nodded. "Me too."

"What you in the mood for?"

He continued to press buttons on the controller. "I don't care to be honest."

He was too busy looking at the television to hear me. Lately I stopped all arguments on things that normally drove me up a wall because I wanted him around to fuck up his life and I couldn't do that if I got on his nerves.

"Some pizza?"

"Okay," he said.

"You hear me, Reggie?"

"Okay."

I rolled my eyes because his response told me he didn't know what I said. Taking a deep breath, I got up and walked outside to get into my car.

Pushing my textbooks off the seat and onto the floor, I opened the glove compartment and got one of the many bands of money I bonded that Russo gave me. Then I made a call.

"Hey, you ready?"

"Yep," Sharon said. "Get the food first though right?"

"Yes, and don't come without it. I already paid for it."

"Damn, 'Mika. Ain't no need to be rude. I just wanna make sure I do this right."

"Listen, you the one who needed the extra paper remember? So I'm doing you a fucking favor and it ain't about being rude."

"Wow, remind me not to get on your bad side. It's like you got two personalities."

"Are you ready or not?"

"Yes, girl, fuck! Now I wish you never spoke to me in class."

"Just get the fucking food and be on the way. I don't want him to leave."

"I got you."

"We need to go over your lines again?"

"Nope. Ready to go."

When she hung up I pulled away from the house. Not that Reggie was looking for me but if he got up and looked out the window I wanted him to see me gone.

Twenty minutes later Sharon showed up wearing tight jeans and a white t-shirt with no bra. I wanted her as appealing as possible. Although she was a cute redbone with long silky hair, he would've fucked a hole in the wall if it was wet and deep enough.

All I'm saying is that I hope this shit works.

REGGIE

I was just about to restart the game when there was a knock at the door. My plan was to never go out again so I could stop fucking everything moving. Even though I couldn't stay in the house forever, I was gonna stay in for as long as possible.

When the doorbell ran again I grew irritated. Where was my wife?

"Tamika!"

DING DONG.

"Tamika, get the door!"

DING DONG.

"Tamika!"

DING DONG.

Fuck, when did she leave the house?

I tossed the controller down and opened the front door. The moment I saw the delivery girl my dick got hard. I looked up and down the block from where I stood for my wife's car.

"You order pizza, sexy?" She said wiping her hair over her left shoulder.

I cleared my throat. "Maybe, uh, like I think my wife may have but I can't be sure."

"Your wife? Well, where is she?"

I ran my hand down my face. "Not sure either."

She smiled harder while the pizza box sat in the palm of her right hand. "Well, I don't wanna overstep but she's a fool for leaving you by yourself. Even for a minute."

"Why you, why you say that?"

"You know what," she paused. "I'm gonna keep my thoughts to myself." She looked at me like she wanted to eat me up.

I looked left and right again. "Listen, how 'bout you come in for a minute."

"Maybe I will." She handed me the pizza and pushed her way inside. I looked left and right again and closed then locked the door behind me.

CHAPTER SIX

TAMIKA

Tears ran down my face as I watched Sharon walk into my house. Yes fucking Reggie was part of the plan but still it hurt.

So much.

No matter what happened I legit still love Reggie, even though I knew he was wrong for me. At the end of the month I married a man who wasn't able to love me and it fucked up my mind.

After pulling myself together and wiping my tears away I grabbed my phone. I dialed a number then waited.

"I'm busy right now, Tamika," Amina said.

"I know and I'm sorry. It's just that I think I left the oven on and I know you were at the house so I wanted you to turn it off for me."

"Girl, ain't nobody at the house. I told you I was taking Naverly to her appointment."

It was obvious that my sister despised me for Reggie so it was always hard talking to her these days. It's like she was losing her mind.

"Oh, I heard a female voice talking to Reggie upstairs and—"

"A FEMALE'S VOICE UPSTAIRS!" She yelled.

"Yeah. But it was probably the TV. You know how Reggie be—"

CLICK.

"Hello."

I looked at the phone and smiled when I saw she hung up. Now all I had to do was wait.

AMINA

"I know but it's not like you ain't with her, Russo." I grabbed my phone and stood up. "Just make sure she healthy and bring her by the house after the doctor examines her."

"Where you going though?" He glared.

I kissed my daughter and walked away from them. Russo and me been over but when he left it gave me the excuse I needed to abandon this marriage.

At first after he told me, when I was alone, I wondered if I still had feelings for Russo. And to my surprise I realized I did. But it wasn't enough to leave Reggie or stop seeing him. I was waiting on the word to be with Reggie fulltime but part of me wondered if he really wanted forever with me?

After running five red lights I finally made it to the house. I saw an unfamiliar car out front and I had all intentions on going ape shit if a female was in my house and with my man.

REGGIE

Her pussy stank a little more than I liked but she was still cute. With the odor I was sure she fucked on the regular despite it being tight.

Her hands were on the sink as I was pumping her hard from behind. Hands gripping her waist. "I'm almost there uh—" I realized I didn't know her name.

"It's Janice," she said as her tongue hung out the side of her mouth.

I grabbed her ass cheeks and lifted up as I pounded harder. I had to be quick because Tamika could come back at any moment. "Yeah, uh, Janice or whatever. Just keep it there."

Right before I bust my nut the door came flying open and Amina pushed inside. Since I hadn't gotten mine yet, I gripped Janice harder as she tried to get away. Amina on her crazy shit pounded the girl on the top of the head.

Seconds later, maybe from all the excitement, I exploded inside of her. When I was good I tucked my dick into my boxers, pulled up my pants and tried to pry Janice from Amina's hands.

"WHAT...THE...FUCK...ARE YOU DOING WITH MY MAN!" Amina continued as she kept hitting her.

"Stop it!" I pushed Amina back and she yanked the girl by the hair.

"FUCK YOU, REGGIE!" She cried. "I HATE YOU! DO YOU HEAR ME? I HATE YOU!"

When I pulled Amina by grabbing her by the waist the girl ran out the bathroom, stepping on the pizza box that sat on the floor on the way out. I brought the box upstairs just in case Tamika came home. I was gonna tell her that I had to get money out my wallet but that didn't happen.

Tamika didn't catch me.

Amina did.

When I heard the door slam I walked toward my room knowing she would follow.

"What is wrong with you?" She screamed as I flopped on the bed. "Why can't you keep your dick in your pants? Why do you have to be so weird?"

I rubbed my temples. "Cut it out."

"Cut it out? Cut it out? That's all you can say to me?"

"Fuck you want me to say? You not my wife!"

"You the worst person in the world, Reggie! You walk around not caring about who you hurt."

"It ain't that."

She flopped next to me. "Then what is it? Talk to me?"

I turned toward her and looked into her eyes. Amina is so fucking pretty, even when she crazy. Or maybe especially when she's like this but I didn't sign up for this shit.

When we first started it was fun but now she putting more weight on me than my wife.

Oh wait.

Where is Tamika?

"Amina, listen…I fuck with you but I can't deal with this right now."

She wiped tears away and her eye makeup smeared all over her face. "You hurt me."

"I know and I'm sorry but you gotta cut this extra shit out."

She sniffled.

"Now Tamika could be on her way in any minute. You want her to see us like this?"

"Like what?"

"Like what?" I paused. "Your makeup smeared, a box of smashed pizza by the bathroom door and—"

"I got it," She said softly.

"Do you?"

"Yeah," she cried.

"Now I love you. And the only one I wanna be with is you but this me sometimes. I like a little something extra but it don't change what's going on with us."

"Reggie, there's gotta be a reason you like this."

KNOCK! KNOCK! KNOCK! KNOCK!

"What the fuck?" I jumped up and looked out the window. What I saw made me shake my head.

Amina walked over to me. "Who is it?"

I looked at her slowly. "The police."

CHAPTER SEVEN

AMINA

I was sitting in a jail cell trying to calm down. My world was different and I felt the most unlike myself I ever had.

"Amina, you can make a phone call," an officer said walking up to the bars.

"Thank you."

When I made it to the phone I called Reggie five times, trying to get him to answer. Each time he didn't pick up. I couldn't call Russo or Tamika because if they found out why I was here, I would be forced to tell them what happened and then explain why I fought a female over my brother-in-law.

FUCK! FUCK! FUCK!

"Inmate, that's it," a police officer said walking up to me. "Time to go back to your cell."

TAMIKA

"Sharon, why would you call the police?" I asked her as I sat in my car.

"I didn't."

"Then who did?"

"I, I don't know," she said wiping tears away. Bruises from my sister's strikes on her face. "But it wasn't me. I know she's Russo's wife and I would never do that. I value life too much."

I exhaled. "Aight, but if I were you I'd keep this between us. Don't tell nobody. You got it?"

"I promise, just, just don't tell Russo okay?"

"Just don't tell nobody else," I repeated before glaring at her.

She was about to leave when she turned around and said, "Tamika."

"What?" I asked as I looked at a text message I received.

"If that was your husband, why was Amina so mad?"

I frowned. "Get out of my car and remember what I said. Tell no one!"

When she was gone I smiled. Not because my heart wasn't broken about Reggie being the man I knew he was, but because I was the one who called the cops. I faked like I didn't know who it was because I didn't want her telling the town what was going down at my house.

But I was behind all this shit.

When I was sure the coast was clear I walked into the house and smelled food cooking. I was choked up. Moving further in, toward the kitchen, I saw Reggie frying chicken.

"Hey you," I said as I spread my fake smile across my face. "You hungry already?"

He cleared his throat. "Uh, why you say that?"

"I ordered some food."

"Oh, so you, you ordered the pizza." He put the fork on the table and walked toward me.

"Yeah."

"It was bad so I threw it out."

Lying ass!

"But why you leave?" He asked me. He wrapped his arms around my waist.

"I needed to pick up my prescription. You know my eczema been bothering me again."

He kissed me. "Let's chill tonight." He paused. "Now go get cleaned up. I'ma eat that pussy all night."

I hated him to death but I did like my cookie eaten. But little did he know, while his head was between my legs and his tongue was on my clit I would be planning my next move.

REGGIE

Tamika was sitting on my face and I was running my tongue in and out of her pussy. I was about to finish off by doing my signature move, which always sent her screaming when I felt my phone vibrating under me. I didn't have to look because I knew who was calling.

Amina.

"Keep it right there," Tamika moaned. "That feels soooo good."

I rolled my tongue over her clit and before I knew it she was shivering as she collapsed her pussy against my mouth. After breathing heavy she crawled off and smiled at me. I made sure my cell was tucked under the covers so she wouldn't notice.

"Why do you do that so good?" She said heavily.

"Because I know what you like."

"Is that right?" She said before yawning. "Because I...I..."

Just that quickly she was snoring.

When she was asleep I slipped out of the bed and grabbed my phone. Standing in the living room, I waited and within fifteen minutes my phone rang again. I looked upstairs to be sure Tamika wasn't coming and then answered.

"Reggie, why you ain't answer my calls?"

"'Mika was—"

"I'm locked up."

I flopped on the sofa. "You sound surprised."

"You gotta come get me. My bail is $1,000."

"And what I'ma tell Tamika when I come back in 11:00 at night with her sister? Huh?"

She sighed. "I can't stay here overnight and it ain't like it's not part your fault anyway."

My teeth gritted. "I'm really not in the mood right now, Amina. I'ma be straight 'bout that shit."

"I know but please come get me," she cried. "I'm scared and I can't spend a night in here."

I rolled my eyes and sighed.

"Please, Reggie!"

An hour and a half later Amina's bail was paid and she was sitting in the passenger seat of my car. Pressing buttons on the radio with an attitude. She was also opening and slamming the glove compartment like she lost her mind.

I knew what she wanted but I didn't wanna give her the satisfaction by asking what was wrong. Amina wanted a fight but I went left on that shit.

"Maybe we should cool off for a little," she said.

"Okay."

She glared at me. "That easy huh?"

"I'm not gonna keep getting into fights with you. If you want it like that it's cool with me."

She sniffled and wiped her eyes with her knuckles. "You don't care 'bout me."

My jaw twitched again and my dick got hard. Not because I wanted her but because I wanted a release. Stress made me horny and I wish I knew why.

"I'm dropping you off." I pulled up down the block, out of view of our house.

"But where you going?"

"Get out." I parked.

"Reggie, look, I'm sorry about—"

"GET THE FUCK OUT!"

She frowned at me; her body shivering and it became obvious she was more into me than I was into her. It was like everything around me was out of control.

She pushed the door open but doubled back. "Since you leaving you won't care about the conversation I'm gonna have with my sister." She glared.

"What that 'spose to mean?"

She smiled. "So now you wanna talk."

"What the fuck did that mean?"

"It means that if you out all night I may get lonely. And when I get lonely I wanna talk. A lot. So since Tamika is the only one home I guess that means—"

"No you won't." I said confidently.

"How you figure?" She frowned.

"You won't tell her for two reasons. First, if you say anything I'll never fuck with you again. With the secret being out the fun will be gone and so will I."

"Whatever, Reg—"

"And the second reason you won't tell is because if my wife finds out before I'm ready to let her know, I'll kill you with my bare hands. You got it?"

She looked down and I shoved her out on the street before pulling off. I needed some new pussy and it was time to go get it.

AMINA

I was making tea to help me go to sleep. Reggie was driving me insane and I told myself over and over to let it go but nothing worked. I couldn't stop wanting and needing him.

"Hey," Tamika said walking into the kitchen while yawning. "I didn't know you were here."

"Just got in."

"You look crazy. You alright?"

I grabbed my teacup and walked out the kitchen. She followed me. "I'm fine." My eyes rolled around the living room before flopping on the sofa. "But uh, where's Reggie?"

Yes I knew he wasn't home but I had a reason for asking.

She shrugged. "I don't know."

"You ain't concerned?"

She laughed. "You so silly, Amina. You know Reggie love me and ain't going no where. So why should I be concerned? He's a grown man and I can't clock his every move."

"You sound awfully sure."

"It ain't that I'm—"

"I be back," I said cutting her off. I sat the cup on the table. "I gotta use the bathroom."

When I made it there I sat on a closed toilet seat and called Reggie ten times. He didn't answer once and the last call went straight to voicemail.

I snatched the cabinet door open under the sink, grabbed the bleach and opened the top. I was about to drink it when I sat it on the floor and cried heavily. I gotta get this man out of my system. He wasn't good for me but where could I start?

When I walked back into the living room I sat down and said, "Call Reggie."

"Why?"

"Tell him to bring me some cigarettes. I'll pay him back when he get here because I ran out. I didn't even know I was on my last one earlier tonight."

She pulled the cell from her pink pajama pants.

After dialing the number she smiled and said, "Hey big head. Why you leave?"

I was furious that he answered for her and not me and it was tough to hide how I felt from my face.

"So your sexy ass gonna put me to sleep and bounce?" She giggled. "You—"

"Are you gonna ask him to get the cigarettes or not?" I snapped. "All that other shit is dumb."

She took the phone from her ear. "You okay?"

"Nah." I looked down. "I just want my cigarettes that's all."

She shook her head. "I don't know why you started that habit again anyway." She said to me as she focused back on the call. "Reggie, can you—"

She paused.

"Okay," she said into the phone.

I moved uneasily on the sofa.

"Okay," she said again.

What was he saying to her?

"I love you too," she continued before hanging up and placing her cell on the sofa.

When the call was over I wanted to know what was said. Already there was a knot in my stomach but I couldn't straight up ask about her marriage.

"You wanna drink with me?" She asked.

"Uh, yeah, but did you tell him about my cigarettes? Because ya'll got off the purpose."

She walked into the kitchen. "He had to go!" She yelled. "Didn't get a chance to ask."

But where?

My sister not caring about her husband was annoying. I needed her to be more aggressive or else Reggie could be out there in the streets doing anything.

When she came back she was carrying a bottle of Kettle One Vodka and two glasses. She wasn't supposed to be drinking since she was a recovering addict but I didn't care at the moment.

I needed relief and for now I needed the company.

CHAPTER EIGHT

REGGIE

I didn't go home last night. Instead I grabbed a hotel and stayed overnight. I knew if I went home Amina would set shit off, we would be fighting and Tamika would hear it all. That's why the moment I heard her voice when I was talking to Tamika I told her I had to go.

"This is not painful," my psychiatrist said. "In fact it's very useful if you can relax into the process."

"You sure?"

He smiled. "Trust me."

I sat back. "I hate that phrase."

He nodded. "I can understand that. And I'm not trying to manipulate you in anyway. I just want you to know that through hypnosis so much more is available to you that the mind is hiding away. We can—"

"Why we doing this though?"

He sighed. "You called me no less than four times this week. Up from last week."

"If you don't want me calling you I won't make an appointment. It ain't nothing but a thing."

"I never said that."

"Then what—"

"You're sick, Reggie. And I think if you can understand that your illness is no less real than cancer or depression, it can help you heal and stop the actions you hate." He got up and dimmed the lights before sitting back down. "Now try and relax."

I wasn't feeling it at all because I knew it wouldn't work.

I didn't want anybody poking around in my head. At the same time...

"Reggie," my psychiatrist said.

I felt heavy. "Yeah."

"Are you okay?"

"Yes, uh, why you say that?"

"We finished the hypnosis session."

I frowned. "But I, I don't remember that."

He smiled. "Well we're done."

I looked around. I felt stupid and irritated that it worked.

"Reggie, can I ask you something?"

I ran my hands down my face. I couldn't believe I went under and had no memory of it. "I guess."

"Where is your mother?"

I frowned. "Why?"

"She may be responsible."

"For what?"

"For more things than you know."

AMINA

I drank too much last night. I probably would've still been asleep but I heard back-to-back knocking on the front door.

"TAMIKA, GET THE DOOR!" I put the pillow over my head.

KNOCK! KNOCK! KNOCK!

I removed the pillow. "TAMIKA!"

When I didn't hear her I got up and rolled out of bed, falling to the floor. Rubbing my knees, I stood up, grabbed my robe off the side of the door and walked downstairs. My temples throbbed with every movement and I couldn't believe I let myself get that drunk.

Once downstairs I walked to the door. "Who is it?"

"We need to speak to Mrs. Amina Jameson." One of the two people said when I opened the door.

I frowned. "Who are you and what's this about?"

"I'm Susan Tuckett with Child Protective Services. And this is very important." She paused. "We have your daughter."

RUSSO

I was in my car with Amina in my passenger seat heated. How the fuck did this bitch lose my kid? She was getting worse than reckless and it had me wanting to go dark.

"I don't know, Russo!" Amina yelled. "We gotta ask her what happened."

"I'm asking you! You her fucking mother!"

"Look, she's old enough to not walk outside by herself. She knows better."

I tried my best not to punch this bitch in her face. She had one job in life and that was to take care of my daughter. It was the only reason she was still alive. I paid all the bills and even kept Reggie's bitch ass on the payroll in a limited way.

Truth was I didn't care anymore that they fucked.

Scratch that.

I didn't care as much.

Sometimes when things were good and I looked at Amina's face when I lived there, I remembered how I felt about her in the beginning. Those were the hardest times for me because it was easier to hate her. It was easier to fake like we never were in love.

But I'm a patient man. And the moment my daughter was eighteen I was gonna kill both of them, which is why I wanted nothing to do with Tamika's childish plan.

An hour later we were meeting with the social workers that agreed to give Naverly to me, especially after I told her I had a home away from my wife. They were still gonna investigate to make sure it was fit but I wasn't worried about that. My home was legit.

In the past I would fight this broad and swear that my wife was a good woman. The kind of woman who would never cheat on me but now I didn't know this slut at all.

"First of all you don't know nothing about me or my daughter!" Amina yelled.

Fuck.

The way she was gearing up I knew things would go left for us getting Naverly back.

"I'm not saying that," the social worker said. "But it's my job to ensure the well being of Naverly. To be sure she won't be harmed now or in the future."

"Amina, relax," I said placing my hand on hers even though I didn't wanna touch her. "We gonna be good."

"That's easy for you to say, you the one getting her."

"How you sound?" I asked. "She's not an object, Amina. She's our child."

"He's right," the social worker said.

"You know what I mean." Amina said.

"I think you should be grateful she's coming with me instead of fighting what's—"

"Oh so I should be happy she's going home to be with a felon?" She laughed.

The social worker frowned. "Come again?"

"My husband was arrested on a drug charge and—"

"Was acquitted," I said finishing her sentence. I mean what was she doing? "All of the charges were dropped."

Amina was taking this shit to another level and I was starting to wonder if she was bipolar or not.

I did know this. If she fucked me out of getting my kid, causing Naverly to be placed in a home, there would be problems for this bitch. Not in some years but days.

"I don't see anything about Mr. Jameson but I do see where you were brought up on charges last night," the social worker said as she thumbed through some paperwork. "Yet another reason why we don't believe you are fit to care for her right now."

I looked at Amina. "What's she talking about?"

"Nothing."

I glared.

"Russo, it was a fight with some bitch who looked at me the wrong way. Nothing for you to be fucking—"

"Language." The social worker said.

Amina rolled her eyes. "Can we talk about this at home?"

"*We* don't have a home," I said.

"You know what I mean, Russo."

I ran my hand down my face and looked at the social worker. "Where can I pick up my daughter?"

She looked at some papers on her desk. "I'll be right back." She stood up and walked out the office.

When we were alone I glared at Amina. "I never give you shit despite everything you did by abusing me when I was in a wheelchair, unable to fight for myself. But I never got over it either."

She rolled her eyes again. "Whatever, Russo."

I grabbed her wrist and squeezed. "I'm out of the chair now, bitch. And if I find out who you fucking is messing with my daughter's well being, then I will kill you."

Amina trembled.

"Okay, Russo," she said softly. "Okay."

CHAPTER NINE

REGGIE

I drove up to the apartment complex my mother lived in. Things weren't as safe as the crib I brought her when we were good and before I cut her off but she had to downgrade.

I pulled up on a group of drunks hugging the block. "Aye, any of yah know Gina?"

They looked at each other and back at me. The bushiest head of the three stepped up to my car. He smelled like the business end of a toilet and I frowned.

"What she look like?" He scratched his head and on everything a bug flew out. "This Gina you asking for."

I described her.

Bushiest looked at his men and then at me. "You talking about Sweet Lips?"

I gripped the steering wheel tight. "That's my mother you talking about, nigga."

"My bad young bull." He said with both palms facing me. "I was just trying to—"

"You know her or not?" I yelled.

His two buddies walked away and when they were gone he took a deep breath. "I'm sorry to tell you this but she was murdered two weeks ago. Didn't you see the news?"

REGGIE

I asked around for the right spot to get what I needed and Bushiest led me to the place. When I found the girl I wanted I pulled up on her and smiled.

She was dark skin with a small mouth and fat ass and I couldn't wait to stick my dick into both. I rolled the window down. "You looking good."

"You wanna trade compliments or do you wanna cum?" Her voice was way deep for a pretty girl like her but it's whatever. I wanted relief and I needed it now.

I unlocked my car. "Get in."

Fifteen minutes later we were pulling up to a motel. She was wearing tights and her pussy lips were fat. I could see them clearly even though they were covered.

Five more minutes later and I was laying on the bed and she was crawling over top of me. My dick was pointed to the ceiling, loaded and ready—

My mother's face popped into my head.

I closed my eyes and tried to push it out.

"Look, honey, I wanna take care of you but you're gonna have to help me out too."

I rubbed my face. "I'm sorry, it's just—"

"I can give you a by the hour rate if you want something a little longer otherwise—"

"No, really, I'm ready."

She winked and crawled on the bed again before grabbing my dick. I was so hard it hurt and at the same time my mother's face flashed into my mind again. It was torture. Her death felt like it was on my hands because I cut her off when she got into it with my wife.

MMMMMMMM. MMMMMM.

Within seconds I realized this bitch was the best. Every time I focused on my mother she would unleash a glob of spit and splatter it on my dick, jerk me a few times and I was back into the room.

"Keep that shit right there," I instructed as I grabbed the back of her head and pumped into her throat.

MMMMM. MMMMMMM.

"I ain't going nowhere," she said between moans as if I was doing it to her.

When she deep throated me I exploded into her mouth.

"You alright?" She asked.

"Yeah, why you say that?"

"Cause you crying."

I wiped my face and noticed she was right. "I paid you so get the fuck out," I said.

She rolled her eyes. "Nigga, you don't have to tell me twice." She grabbed her purse. "I don't know what your problem is but you better get it together."

TAMIKA

I was at Murphy, my sponsor's house, talking to Russo on the phone. Sitting on his workbench in the basement, I was trying to hide my pleasure.

"I mean, I know she's your sister and everything but—"

"You don't have to fake with me, Russo." I said. "I get it."

"I started to hurt her for real."

"So what you gonna do? About Naverly?"

"See that's what I haven't thought about yet." He paused. "Where you at? You home?"

I knew he was going to ask me that. This is why I specifically wanted to be here. I knew he would ask me to watch my niece. But it was my duty to make sure my sister was uncomfortable and mad enough to make Reggie uncomfortable too.

So as much as I liked Russo he was on his own. Otherwise all that work I put in by getting my sister drunk and letting my niece outside, while I watched her of course, would have been in vain.

"Nah, I'm over a friend's."

"Oh, cause I was gonna ask if you could get Naverly for me today."

"I would but Murphy wanna take me out and I been putting him off for the longest."

"Ain't he your sponsor?"

I frowned. "How you know that?"

"You told me. You don't remember?"

I didn't.

"I remember everything you tell me because I give a fuck about you, Tamika."

I smiled.

"But let me leave you to it," he said. "Stop by and see a nigga when you get a chance. Just cause we don't live together no more don't mean I don't fuck with you."

"Okay, I will." I hung up.

"What you doing?" Murphy said coming down the steps.

"Was talking to Russo."

He nodded. "Still on your revenge shit?"

I frowned. "That's why I don't tell people nothing. Quick to throw it up in your face when the time is bad."

"Not doing that."

I walked over to him. "My sister's fucking my husband. Don't I deserve a little relief?"

"Yes." He sighed.

"So what's the problem?"

"You know I don't like Ole boy."

"You mean my husband?"

"Yeah. Especially after he broke my jaw. But you don't want none of what he got going on to push you back to drugs or suicide."

"Won't happen."

"How you know, Tamika?"

"Because I'm angry and not sad. That's the difference."

"If you aren't careful somebody will get hurt. Isn't that enough to stop what you doing?"

"Not really," I shrugged. "As long as it's not me."

CHAPTER TEN

REGGIE

"My wife thinks I'll fuck anything," I smiled although I felt like crying inside. "Said if it's wet I'll pound it." I continued talking to my psychiatrist. "I wonder if she's right."

"It is tough to understand."

"She doesn't know about what I'm going through. I don't even know."

"Reggie, it's not always easy to—"

"I had sex with a man," I blurted out. "I mean...I think it was because..." the words got trapped in my throat.

He moved uneasily. "Are you gay?"

"No. I mean, I had an idea when I picked her up that something was wrong but..." I wiped my hands down my face. "I been..." I took a deep breath. "I needed a release. So I guess she was right after all."

"Most addicts will do what they have to do to get their high. Sex addiction is no different and it doesn't make you—"

"My mother was murdered."

"When? And how?"

"Recently."

"Are you okay?"

"I just found out yesterday."

He nodded.

"I went looking for her because I, I wanted to ask some questions about..."

"Our session."

I nodded.

He took a deep breath. "Before that session you didn't remember your mother being responsible for your first sexual experience."

"No."

He made some notes on a sheet, something he hardly ever did. "What do you recall, Reggie?"

"It's like that entire period, with all those moments, were wiped out of my mind."

"Did you want to talk about the moments? Because we didn't go into any detail."

I nodded yes.

He took a deep breath and I wondered if my case was weighing heavy on him because he looked stressed. "Based on our hypnosis session your mother used sex to make you feel better."

My heart thumped and I nodded slowly, trying not to pass out. "Did she...did she uh..."

"What?"

"Molest me or—"

"No!" he yelled, palms in my direction.

It wasn't until that moment that I realized I wasn't breathing. "G...good."

"There was a babysitter...much older than you I believe. Anna I think was her name."

All of a sudden a lot of it came back. I sat back and nodded. "Yeah, I do...I remember her now."

"Well based on what you said, she walked in on you giving," he cleared his throat. "On you giving the sitter oral sex."

I searched my mind for that moment and was coming up short. And then I remembered more.

Actually everything.

"My mother had it rough in her, in her relationships and she was always gone. Never home and I remembered staying in the house alone for days at a time. If she had money she would call the sitter if not I would be by myself."

"Did she ever say where she was going?"

"Nah. It could be anywhere. Everywhere." I paused. "Sometimes she was gone and would be home."

"I don't understand."

"Her mind would be elsewhere."

He nodded.

"I would get sad and to make me feel better she would have Anna come over like I said...and we would play."

"I see."

"I didn't even know she knew we were having sex until I overheard my mother telling Anna to make me feel better, sexually. It was the last day before she left for her longest time up to that point."

"Your mother?"

"Yes."

"Where did she go that time?"

"Away. In the streets."

"I see." He nodded.

"I guess my mother was doing me a favor by letting Anna have sex with me because I learned a lot."

"You keep using the word sex and it's important to realize you were molested."

"But I wasn't though."

"Anna was a twenty-one year old woman."

I stared at him. "I told you that too?" I asked softly.

He nodded.

"That's enough for today." I got up and walked out.

"REGGIE!" He yelled. "REGGIE, COME BACK!"

AMINA

I really can't believe my life

Reggie wouldn't answer my

getting annoyed with him at this

I asked my sister if she talked to h

if she could care less and said no.

Something is up with Tamika.

For real.

I'm really starting to wonder if she ever loved him to begin with, or if she knows about us and doesn't care. But every time I try to believe it, that she knows, I remember how much she cried when back in the day he threatened to leave her forever. And then I realize she couldn't possibly know because she would be devastated.

What would be the reason to let me sleep with him without saying anything?

I called Reggie again and surprisingly he answered. "What?"

at?" I repeated with an attitude. "Why you

act like I'm bothering you or something?"

"You called for a reason so are you gonna tell

me or do you want me to hang up in your face?"

I could feel tears welling up in my eyes. My

little girl lived with her father now. My husband

left me and the one man in the world I wanted to

help me get past this shit didn't care.

What was I going to do?

"Hello?" He yelled.

"Reggie, I'm going through a lot right now." I

paused. "And all I wanna know is if, well, if we

still good. Because I don't think I could handle it

if we weren't."

"I'll talk to you about that later." He said. "But

since you asking I'ma be straight up, I think we

through."

CHAPTER ELEVEN

TAMIKA

I couldn't believe I spent two nights over Murphy's house. I would've been still asleep if Reggie hadn't been blowing up my phone. He doesn't know that I know he spent a night out the other day because I didn't say a word to him when he texted me.

Not comin home. Need 2 B by myself.

Usually that would send me on the edge but I responded:

Take all the time you need.

He called me multiple times after that but I wouldn't answer which forced him into a text convo with me, which he hated. In the end he told me how much he loved me. I answered each one as if everything was good but I never answered the phone when he called.

Part of my reason was to make things uncomfortable and I knew if he was unsure of what was going on with me he would lose his mind and that is exactly what happened when he returned home after his FUCK FEST and found out I didn't come back.

"Hello," I said yawning finally answering his call.

"Fuck are you?" Reggie yelled.

"Excuse me?" I said calmly.

"You stayed out all last night and didn't tell me, Tamika! What...you mad because I wanted one night out and you playing get back or something?"

"Of course not," I said rolling over in bed. "I want you at peace, Reggie."

"Fuck does that mean, Tamika?"

"Why do you wanna argue?"

"You my wife!"

This nigga is a whole FUCKING MESS.

"I know and I'm happy to be."

Silence.

"Reggie." I smiled knowing he was heated but had no room to be mad at me staying out since he had too. "Are you okay?"

"I want you home by the end of the day or else, Tamika. Straight up."

I smiled. "Or else what?"

He sighed. "Just, just come home. Please."

When I hung up with him I rolled back over with a smile on my face only to see Murphy standing at the door with his arms crossed over his chest.

"What?" I said sitting up.

He came in and sat on the edge of the bed. "What is going on with us? I mean really."

I kissed him on the cheek and smiled. "What you mean?"

"Are we together or not?"

Oh, this dude is serious. I sighed, "I like you."

"So why don't you wanna have sex?"

I frowned. "Is that all you care about?"

"How you sound?"

"I'm a married woman."

"I know this, Tamika."

"Do you really?" I stared into his eyes. "You gotta give me some time, Murphy. For real."

He could kill himself if he didn't understand.

How he gonna put the pressure on me when he knew what I was going through? Like I didn't hear him talking shit behind my back when he was trying to get Reggie mad a while back.

Nah, I liked him but I was done with letting men play me in this lifetime. I was done with drugs too, which made him useless.

Things would definitely be on my time from here on out.

AMINA

I was sitting across from April at the kitchen table while she stared down my throat. "Why though?" She asked me.

"You gotta ask Russo why he left. I don't have the answers."

She sat in the chair. "I know you."

"What that mean?"

"You know why he left. Now are you gonna tell me or not? Because this ain't adding up."

Something told me to keep my secret to myself but I needed to tell somebody about what was going on in my world or I would explode. So I chose her.

"I really don't know why Russo left but there is a reason I don't care."

"I'm listening."

"Me and Reggie together." I said smiling, my hands together in front of me.

She frowned. "What that mean?"

"We together." I put my hands flat on the table.

Silence.

"Say something, April," I said.

"You not talking about your sister's husband are you?"

"No." I frowned.

"I was about to—"

"I'm talking about my man."

She shook her head slowly from left to right. "No, no, no, no, no, Amina. You can't do this!"

I fanned the air. "Oh so you gonna act like you didn't fuck my boyfriend?"

"Amina, I was messed up in the head and—"

"So am I!"

"But you have so much going on for you."

"How you figure?" I paused. "I mean what is so fucking perfect about my life?"

"You have a house that's paid off, a daughter who loves you to pieces and—"

"Nobody to love me! Reggie is the only person who really sees me."

She took a deep breath and I wished I never said a word to this bitch. "You gonna hurt your sister more than you ever can imagine if you do this and she finds out."

"I am doing this and she doesn't care." I paused. "At least that's how she acts when it comes to Reggie."

"I doubt that."

"April, I didn't tell you to be judged. I told you to let you know what's happening in my life since you say we don't talk."

She grabbed her purse and stood up. "The worst thing I did was fuck your nigga. And now I feel bad about it. But if you continue to do what you're doing somebody's gonna get hurt. Maybe beyond repair."

She walked out.

FUCK THAT BITCH!

Little did she know I had plans on telling Tamika about us tonight. And there was nothing anybody could do to stop me.

Not even Reggie.

RUSSO

"What's up?" I asked Reggie when he walked up to the driver's side of my car. "You got me here. Now what's so important that it couldn't wait 'til tomorrow?"

Reggie frowned. "You 'aight?"

My jaw twitched.

I was humoring this nigga for my kid until her eighteenth but being fake was weighing on me.

"You called me and said you wanted something so here I am, Reggie." I paused. "What's up?"

"You talk to Tamika?"

"What, nigga?" I glared. "You got me all the way out here to ask me did I speak to your wife?" I pointed at him.

He stepped back. "Russo, if I did something wrong to you let me know."

This dude was really trying me. And I vowed to do nothing about it. Right now my daughter was with April and if I didn't have her I'd be fucked up out here in these streets. Her and her husband were good people and I appreciated it because this nigga and my wife were crumbs.

"You know what, man," I pulled off an left him looking stupid in the street.

REGGIE

Fuck wrong with that dude? He acted like I did something to—

I slid in my car.

He knows.

He knows about Amina and me and that means Tamika knows too. This was gonna fuck up everything. But why didn't he step to me if that was true? I knew Russo and if he knew I wouldn't be alive.

I had to get home.

When I made it to the house Tamika was in the living room watching TV and Amina was in the kitchen. I busted a left and sat next to my wife on the sofa.

"What you doing?"

She smiled and kissed me softly on the lips as if everything was okay. "Hey you."

I tried to look into her eyes to see if I could read her but I was coming up short. This shit was fucking me up. Did she know or not?

"Can I talk to you?"

She sat back. "Sure, Reggie. Is everything cool? You look like something's heavy on your mind."

Suddenly I felt Amina staring at me. When I glanced up she was standing in the doorway. "Can I talk to you both?" Amina asked.

My heart thumped.

Please don't do this, I pleaded with her with my eyes.

Tamika looked at Amina and then at me. "Is everything okay?" She paused. "You guys look serious."

Amina grinned and walked away.

"What was that about?" Tamika asked me while laughing.

I shrugged.

I knew Amina had intentions on fucking up my world and she was gonna make me bust her in the mouth if she kept playing games. "I wanted to ask if you were good."

"Reggie," she nudged my leg. "You asked me that already."

She was right.

Amina had my head fucked up and had me forgetting shit. Russo too for that matter.

"Have you talked to Russo?"

"Yeah."

"When?" I frowned.

"Earlier today."

My stomach jumped. "That's good."

"Reggie, you're scaring me."

I took a deep breath. "Listen," I grabbed her hand. "Things may be off but they gonna get better. I'm...I'm making some mistakes but—"

"Reggie," she put her hand on the side of my face. "I have no doubt that things are gonna work out just right with us."

"What that mean?"

"It means I love you. And I know you were uncomfortable when I stayed out all night but it's not because I don't love you." She kissed me on the lips and smiled. "Now I'll be right back."

What I knew in the moment was this, I couldn't do life without my wife.

But first I had to get rid of Amina. Which was gonna be easier said than done.

CHAPTER TWELVE

REGGIE

"What were you about to do?" I asked Amina as I gripped both of her arms in the middle of her bedroom. "Why you being hot and shit downstairs?"

"Hot?" She said with wide eyes. "Try love."

"If you loved me you wouldn't try to ruin my life, Amina! You really pushing me against the wall."

"Reggie, whatever." She wiggled out of my grasp and slid down to the floor. I yanked her back to her feet.

"I'm not fucking around with you."

She snatched away from me again. "What is your plan then, Reggie? Huh? Because mine is to sit down Russo and Tamika and tell them everything about us."

"Why though?"

"So we don't have to hide anymore!" She yelled. "So we can see what it's like to finally be together and not hide like rats! You keep asking me the same thing and my answer will never change. I want it to be just us."

This bitch is crazy.

Yes, I told her I wanted forever but I never had any intentions on actually leaving Tamika. My mind was always on sex and whatever I could say to get her to keep fucking me. I hoped we would get tired of each other at the same time and get back to normal but this shit...

"What can I do to convince you not to do that?"

She smiled.

She knew she had me right where she wanted me.

"Cut all things off."

"Amina, stop—"

"I'm serious! No other bitches. No fucking other females on the side and no leaving me alone and not coming home."

"Amina, you can't—"

"I'm not done!" She threw a finger in my face.

I glared. "'Go 'head."

"And no Tamika."

I backed up. "Not possible."

She moved closer. "It's not possible because she's still in the picture."

"Because I still—"

"Don't say it," she said. "That's gonna make me get in my car and go find Russo and Tamika to tell—"

"You really over here blackmailing me," I frowned. "I can't believe this shit."

"I'ma do what I have to do to keep you and there ain't nothing that you can do, short of killing me that will ever change that."

REGGIE

"I fucked up," I told my psychiatrist.

"Explain."

"I'm gonna lose my wife and it wasn't until today that I really, really understood what it could mean for me."

He nodded. "Tell her." He paused. "Tell her everything right now, Reggie."

"You mean about Amina and me?"

"Yes."

"Can't do that."

"If you don't get out in front of this and come as clean as you can, you will lose her and more."

"She won't stay."

"You can't say that. But she does deserve an opportunity to prove you wrong."

"I think Amina is crazy."

"I hate that term."

"That's cause this is your field."

"No. There's always a reason for things that appear as you say, crazy." He paused. "Did anything happen to her?"

"Not that I..."

"What is it?"

"Her brother just died and before that her mother." I ran my hand down my face. "And she's married but he was violent at one point and...and—"

"She's afraid of abandonment." He paused. "I don't know how close she was to her brother and mother but back to back losses without a release can make some lose their mind."

"There something else," I paused. "That's major."

"What?"

"When her mother was on her dying bed I was in the room. And I, I promised to take care of her and my wife."

He sat back and smiled. "That's it. And she's unconsciously holding you to it."

REGGIE

I just finished my set in the gym when I felt somebody grilling me from behind. When I looked over it was April."

I smiled at her and she rolled her eyes and walked out the door.

What the fuck?

I put the dumbbell down and jogged behind her, catching her in the parking lot. "April, what's up?"

She kept walking.

"Hold up."

I ran behind her and gripped her hand. "You heard me?"

She snatched away. "I don't talk to foul ass niggas these days."

"What?" I frowned.

"How you gonna fuck both of my cousins in the same house? Huh, Reggie?"

AMINA! That bitch told her.

She tripping like shit. Why would she tell her when she know how close she is to Tamika?

"It's not like that."

She crossed her arms over her chest. "I'm sorry, but did your dick accidently fall into Amina's pussy?"

"Something like that."

"You know what..." She turned to walk away and I grabbed her hand again before letting it go.

"Bad joke?"

"Worse than that."

"I know," I paused. "I know but, well, it's complicated, April. And I know you don't understand but its true,"

"But why, Reggie?" She said softly. "You were one of the good ones. I always liked you. What happened to you?"

All I could think was that I was glad I didn't try to fuck this girl. She would've went straight to Tamika. I guess the doctor saving me after all.

"I'm gonna end this, April."

She frowned. "That ain't what I heard."

"What you mean?"

"Amina is under the impression that she is about to assist you in breaking my little cousin's heart."

"Nah."

"Whatever you got into I know this, either you tell Tamika what's up or I'ma do that for you." She stormed off.

FUCK!

AMINA

I can't believe he would do this to me!

I'm sitting in the parking lot of the gym watching my cousin stab me in the back by talking to Reggie. I couldn't trust that whore with my boyfriend in high school and I'm realizing I can't trust her now.

Picking up my phone I decided to make a call. I blocked my number and the phone rung twice before April's husband answered. "Yep, who's this?" He asked.

"Your wife is a red whore. And you better talk to her."

"Hold up, who the fuck is—"

CLICK.

I said all that needed to be said to him. Now it was time to make my actions speak for themselves since Reggie thought it was a game.

When I made it home I walked straight into Reggie and Tamika's room. Standing in the middle of the floor I took a deep breath. There was so much that needed to be done and I had no other choice.

Besides, it was obvious of what had to go down. I needed to get rid of every bitch in or around my man willingly or not. It really didn't make a difference.

I ran back downstairs and grabbed a trash bag. Walking back into their room I opened the closet door and focused on all Tamika's shit. In less than ten minutes all of her things were in bags and sitting at the front door.

I know this may seem harsh but it was evident to me.

Reggie had too many choices.

He had me.

He had April.

And he had my sister.

The way I looked at it was simple. There was this restaurant around the corner from my house. Whenever I went they handed me a twenty-page menu and I always felt overwhelmed. In the end I end up ordering the same thing.

Chicken fingers and fries.

Whether Reggie wanted to believe it or not I was his chicken fingers and fries and if he didn't know what he wanted I would have to order for him.

When I was done I grabbed what was left of the vodka, a cup and ice. Sitting on the sofa I was feeling good and then...

KNOCK. KNOCK. KNOCK.

"Who is it?" I yelled.

"Ya husband!"

I rolled my eyes and drank down half of what was left. When I was done I walked to the door.

KNOCK. BANG. KNOCK. BANG.

I yanked it open. "Fuck wrong with you?"

"Your daughter wants to see you." Russo said.

"I called twenty times and she didn't want to talk to me once." I held back the tears that were trying to take me over. "What changed all of a sudden?"

"She's a kid."

"And?" I paused taking a swig of vodka. "I'm her mother."

"Amina."

"Amina what?" I paused. "You turning my daughter against me and it's wrong."

RING. RING. RING.

I looked at my phone on the couch.

"Amina," Russo said. "I need you to get yourself together. We got a kid and—"

"I know."

"Do you? Because you out here making fucked up moves and it's messing with—"

RING. RING. RING.

I looked at my phone again. It was probably April blowing up my spot because I called her little husband. She could fuck with me if she wanted but I was not about the games.

"You a mess," Russo said.

I rolled my eyes.

"You on drugs or something?" He asked.

I laughed.

"Fuck is so funny?" He continued "You not taking anything serious."

"You know what, Russo," I paused. "Drugs are the furthest thing from my mind. I'm not my sister so don't get us confused."

"Wow."

"Relax, I know she's so precious to you."

He took a deep breath. "It's gonna be a long time until you see your daughter. And when you finally realized you fucked up by not seeing her today, I want you to remember this."

RING. RING. RING.

I slammed the door in his face and walked to my cell phone. Taking a deep breath I said, "Hello."

"Amina, why did you call my husband saying—"

CLICK.

It was my cousin and I wasn't about to waste my time on her. I made my decision when I decided to give her man a piece of my mind for fucking with mine and now I was done.

My only goal was to wait for Reggie.

We had a lot to discuss.

CHAPTER THIRTEEN

TAMIKA

Reggie wanted to take me out but I told him I wasn't hungry. He seemed disappointed at first but we decided to sit at the park, eat sunflower seeds and watch the sun go down instead.

"I want to tell you something, Tamika," he said as he turned his body on the bench to look at me.

I spit out a shell and focused on him.

The last thing I wanted was Reggie telling me about my sister and them being together. Things were still on my time and I had a few other moves up my sleeves.

"Before you say anything, Reggie let me say something." I put the bag of seeds on my lap. "I am so proud of you. Really proud."

He frowned. "For what?"

"Because I see how you changed."

He readjusted in his seat. "Bae, I think you got me confused with another nigga because—"

"Nope. I'm talking about you."

He sat back. "But how?"

"I remember you telling me that if I just relaxed and not complain about stupid things that everything would be alright." I gripped his hand tight so he could buy everything I was selling his ass. "And I love you so much."

"I love you too but—"

"Listen, I have a good feeling about us. And as long as you stay like this and remain faithful we will be great. I know it in my heart that we will survive, Reggie."

He looked down and took a deep breath.

Got 'em. I could tell by the look on his face. And now let me clean up a little more.

"Reggie," I put my hand on his leg. "You feel okay?"

Silence.

"Reggie..."

"Uh, yeah, I'm, I just got some things on my mind but you're right." He kissed my cheek. "We'll be okay."

REGGIE

"What do you want, boy?" April said when she met me a few blocks away from my house. "Because I don't have a lot of time to be spending on you. My day already crazy."

I was standing on the driver side of her car. "Can I get in at least so we can talk?"

"Why?"

"Please?"

She took a deep breath and unlocked the door. "Come in."

I slid into her passenger seat.

"Did you tell her yet?" She asked.

"That's what I wanted to meet with you about." I paused. "And before you blow up hear me out."

"Get on with it, Reggie." She turned the car on. "Because I'm already irritated."

I turned her car back off. "Please just listen." I took a deep breath. "I tried to tell her about me and Amina. That's actually where I just came from. I even took her somewhere private to—"

"Are you about to tell me you tried and couldn't?" She paused. "Because my husband is waiting on me and—"

"She said if I'm unfaithful it's over. And I know you're angry but I can't tell her if I know off the top she's gonna cut me off." I touched her hand but she snatched away. "I'm sorry, I just...look, if she leave me that's it for me."

"You should've realized that before you fucked Amina."

"But it's not like you think!"

She frowned. "Hold up...are you asking me to validate this shit? Because if you are it ain't happening."

I wiped my hand down my face. "April, please try and see things my way."

"I saw things your way when I didn't tell my cousin after I first found out. I even chose to see things your way when you begged me to be quiet but now," she sighed. "Just get out and leave me out of it, Reggie. Please."

"Does this mean you won't say anything?"

"Just get out!"

My fist crawled up and she looked at me. "Wait, are you gonna, hit me or something?"

I looked down at my hands, opened the door, got out and closed it. Seconds later she peeled off. Something told me I didn't hear the last of her. I was gonna need a miracle to keep that bitch quiet but there wasn't one in sight.

AMINA

I just watched my cousin spend time in the car alone with my man.

I mean what is up with these females? Damn, why can't they keep their hands off of what doesn't belong to them?

Reggie is mine and I was gonna sit by and watch him be snatched away by my whorish cousin? Not again. This time I was gonna fight at all cost and I was gonna win too.

But first I had to deal with my sister and went straight home. I smiled when I saw Tamika sitting on the sofa looking at her shit that I kindly packed.

"Amina, what, what is all this?" She asked going through one of the bags. She stopped and looked at me. "I'm confused."

"Don't be." I shrugged. "It's time for you to get out."

She frowned. "What you talking about? The last thing I remember is that I lived here too."

"Nah, not really."

She stood up. "When Russo paid off the house he put it in our names. I don't have to go anywhere."

I dipped into the kitchen and came back with the deed. "Feel free."

"What's this?"

"Look at it."

She took it from my hand and read it. "So what?" She shrugged. "Legally I can't be thrown out."

"Legally you can play games if you want but trust me you don't want to, Tamika. I already checked and found out I need to get an eviction notice. But if you make me do that I will make your life a living hell."

She took a deep breath. "Can you at least tell me what I did wrong?"

"Nah. Just go."

"Amina, you owe me that much. You may have your document but I thought at the end of the day we were still sisters. You think mama would like to see us like this?"

I looked down and back at her. I hadn't thought about what I would say if she asked why

I wanted her gone. I didn't even think she would bring up mama. I had all intentions on throwing her out by the hair but if I could avoid the scene with words instead I wanted to do that.

"I know you been talking to Russo behind my back, Tamika. And you don't have to lie."

She glared at me and something changed on her face. I can't explain it but it was like I was looking at a whole different person. Someone who could do me harm if I let her.

But then she blinked a few times and turned back into the weak sister I knew was there. "I noticed all of my things are packed but not my husband's. Is there any reason why?"

I walked over to a bag and pulled out a sweatshirt. I had prepared for that question. "What's this then if it isn't Reggie's?"

"Reggie has way more stuff than—"

"Are you gonna leave or get on my nerves? Because we can do whatever."

She walked to the door. "This is not over. I'll be back and you better be careful." She walked out.

CHAPTER FOURTEEN

TAMIKA

"**M**y sister is fucking tripping." I told Murphy as he grilled a couple of steaks in his backyard. "She actually faked like she wasn't the one in the wrong."

"Maybe it's a good thing." He shrugged.

"You sound dumb."

He put the fork down, grabbed my hand and walked me to the picnic table. "You know you can stay here right?"

I sighed. "That's not what I'm saying. Like for real, my sister getting away with everything. She slept with my husband! Had I done that to Russo it would've been—"

"Let me rephrase myself."

I pulled my hand away softly. "Okay."

"I want you here with me."

"But now is not the time to—"

"So what you gonna do?" He said louder. "Stay with Russo?"

"Stay with Russo?" I laughed. "I'm not thinking about that at all right now."

He smirked. "Yeah, 'aight, Tamika."

I looked at him and crossed my arms over my chest. "Meaning?"

"I know you know that he wants to fuck you. I mean how fucked up is your family? Really? Your sister with Reggie, Russo wanting to be with you." He shook his head as if he had us all figured out. "What are ya'll swingers or something?"

I dropped my hands at my sides. "That's not fair."

"Nah, what's not fair is this game you playing with me. I mean, I didn't say anything at first but now-"

"I let you know from the gate that I wanted to take it slow, Murphy. So why you acting like you got amnesia?"

He got up. "You a fucking tease."

"And you psycho."

"You know what, take your shit and get out my house, slut," he said pointing over my head.

I couldn't believe he was going off. Like he was really coming at me like I did something wrong. Actually I should have known he was like this since he had shown himself before and got punched in the jaw by Reggie a while back.

"I'm leaving anyway, nigga," I yelled. "Got a glimpse of your little dick when you left the door open in the bathroom and I wasn't impressed."

"Your pussy stank!"

I tossed the fuck you finger up and walked out the yard. I dodged the bullet with him. I am so glad I still had a lot of the money Russo gave me cause now I could use it to get a place of my own.

While he continued to yell at my back I made a decision. If Amina thought she was gonna stay in that house with Reggie she didn't know me at all. I had plans to burn it to the ground and that's exactly what I was gonna do."

REGGIE

When I walked through the front door I was shocked when I saw a bunch of bags on the floor. I looked through a few of them and saw a couple of my things but most of the shit belonged to my wife.

"Hey, bae," Amina said walking up behind me. "I thought that was you."

"What's going on?"

She walked around the front of me. "I made a line in the sand."

I frowned. "What, bitch?"

She blinked. "I put my sister out."

I backed up. My breath caught in my throat. Here I was trying to get out of this shit and Amina pushed off without my consent. "You...did...what?"

"I had to because—"

"Wait, so she, she knows about us?" I felt my heart rocking and I could see my marriage crashing down. I don't know what I thought would happen when I started with Amina but I definitely didn't see this.

"No!"

"Then what *is* going on?"

"I told her she had to leave and to save our secret for now, I put a couple of your things in the bag too." She smiled. "To fake like I wanted you out with her."

"Where's the rest of my stuff?" I glared.

"In my closet."

Oh my, God. This bitch is really insane. She actually thinks that I would be with her after she pulled this move. Without me even knowing. I was so mad I was trying not to choke her out.

This can't be life.

"Where is she now?" I felt my nostrils flaring.

SILENCE.

"WHERE THE FUCK IS SHE?"

"Does it matter?" She cried.

"Amina, let me make things clear for you. There is no us without her! You get what I'm saying?"

"So, you—"

"Don't say the same shit over and over again! I already told you what was up and—"

"But you changing up!" She cried harder. "When you inside of me it's like you ready to give up the world but now..."

"What exactly did you tell my wife?"

"Who cares?"

"FUCK DID YOU SAY?"

She cried harder.

"You know what, fuck this shit." I turned to walk to the kitchen. Grabbing my phone out of my pocket I dialed Tamika's cell phone. When I got her voicemail I cleared my throat. "Hey, you. I came home and saw our clothes in the living room. You leaving me or something?" I joked. "Call me back so we can talk about this."

I took a deep breath and opened the back door. What am I going to do with this situation? I didn't see a way out.

I was about to walk back toward the living room when suddenly I felt a sharp pain in the back of my head. When I turned my neck, right before dropping to the floor, Amina was standing over top of me holding a bat smiling.

CHAPTER FIFTEEN

TAMIKA

I just filled up a red gas can at the station and put it in my trunk. My plan was simple. I was going to burn the house I had come to love to the ground. Just thinking about it going up in flames gave me chills.

Reggie had been calling and leaving messages but I wouldn't answer, besides, he wasn't saying anything I wanted to hear. As far as I was concerned he was the reason my sister and I weren't getting along and had he never fucked her this would never have happened. Instead he faked like he had no idea that they were planning to throw me out of my home and I hated him for it.

Now that I think about it taking me to the park was probably to tell me that he wanted to run off with my sister and I hated him even more for it.

Yep, they were gonna feel me after I put their sex haven up in flames.

REGGIE

I was laying on the floor of the kitchen, the back of my head throbbing. When I touched the wound it only had a little blood.

"Oh my, god!" Amina said walking up to me with a bag of ice. "You're up."

I rubbed my head. "What are you...what are you doing?" My voice was low and my throat felt dry.

"I know and I'm sorry but—"

"You hit me, 'Mina. With a bat."

"Because you wouldn't listen."

"That's not what you do to people you say you love!" I rubbed my head again. "I mean fuck is wrong with you?"

"That's not fair, Reggie!" She said with wild crazy eyes. "You gave me no choice."

"Oh my, god, you crazy, you really crazy," I kept chanting.

She stooped down and sat by my head. "I only hit you a little bit."

"A...little...fuck is wrong with you?"

"Reggie, calm down because we have to talk. We have to get things together so we'll be on the same page." She placed the ice bag on my head and I tossed it across the kitchen. "Don't be that way."

"Amina, what do you want from me? Right now?"

She smiled and looked even weirder. Like she was psychotic or something. Now that I think about it I don't know why I'm surprised. She did this same thing to Russo when he couldn't walk and was in the wheelchair. So why did I think it wouldn't happen to me?

"I want you to call my sister and tell her you want to be with me. And I want you to leave my cousin alone too."

Silence.

"Reggie, did you hear me?"

"I did." I said through clenched teeth.

"Well?"

"You know my answer."

"I do but I was hoping you'd change your mind." She touched my face and I slapped her hand away. "Considering your condition and all."

"You mean you knocking me in the head?" I paused. "When I wasn't looking?"

"Yeah, that part."

I sat up. "Amina, I, I will do whatever you saying but not now."

"But that's just it. It has to be now."

I rubbed my temples. "Let's talk about—"

KNOCK. KNOCK. KNOCK.

We both looked toward the front door even though we couldn't see it.

KNOCK. BANG. KNOCK.

She looked at me. "You better go get that," I said.

She glared. "Don't move." She stood up and looked down at me. "Or I'll do more than what I just did."

I nodded.

The moment she hit the corner I tried to get up but I had to sit back down. I was afraid of not having my legs under me after she hit me, which is why I didn't move. I felt dizzy but there was no way I could stay on this floor.

As I focused on who was at the door I heard Russo's voice. I started to call his name but then I would have to explain what was going on with his wife and me so I couldn't do that.

So for now I just listened.

"But I need you to," Russo said.

"And I'm telling you like I told you before that I can't do it right now."

"But she's your fucking daughter and April ain't answering my calls."

"Look, just bring her back later, Russo."

"When?"

"I don't know, maybe in a couple of hours."

Wow. I was really turned off by her now. She wasn't even trying to get her own kid. Man, I had to get away from this bitch, a.s.a.p.!

When she came back in she sat next to me and smiled. "Now, we are alone again." She touched my face with her knuckles. "Where were we?" She paused. "Oh, I remember, you were gonna tell my sister that you didn't want to see her anymore."

I smiled and yanked her by the hair. When I had her in my grasp I punched her repeatedly in the face until she passed out.

CHAPTER SIXTEEN

TAMIKA

"I don't know what's going on, April." I said as I looked into her eyes. We were standing in her kitchen and she was wearing her workout clothes. "But Amina isn't acting right. And I'm afraid she's going to do something terrible." My plan was to put the fire I intended to create on my sister and my cousin would be my alibi.

She cleared her throat. "Why," she cleared her throat again. "Why you think she acting weird?"

"That's just it, it doesn't make any sense. She told me she packed my clothes because she wanted to be alone and, and now I'm here talking to you." I paused. "It's like she lost what was left of her mind."

"Well, maybe she feels guilty about something and doesn't want you around."

OH NO.

When I decided to meet her before burning down the house my reason was selfish. I needed April to say that after speaking with me that Amina was tripping and in the end Amina would be set up for the fire. I didn't stop to think that somebody would have told her about the affair. I had to back track out of this.

"I don't know about that," I said clearing my throat.

She bit her bottom lip. "But she may be struggling with some things and...and it's hard for her to tell you."

"This seems more mental to me."

She took a deep breath. "I, uh, I want to tell you something."

At first I was going to cut her off so I wouldn't have to hear about the affair but I came up with an idea. Maybe if I let her tell me what I already know, it would explain even more why Amina burnt down the house."

"What is it?"

"I want you to be calm when I tell you what I'm about to say." She touched my arm. "Okay?"

"You're scaring me." I looked horrified as I stared into her eyes. I was doing my best fake performance. "What's going on?"

"It's about Amina and Reggie."

I sat down at her kitchen table and she sat next to me. "What about them?"

She took a deep breath. "They having an affair."

I put my hand over my heart.

And then the top of my head.

And then my stomach.

"Hold up," she said pointing at me. "You knew didn't you?"

Oh, fuck! "What are you talking about?"

She squinted and looked harder at me and I looked away. "I know how to read fakeness when I see it."

I took a deep breath.

When I set out to make my cousin my accomplice I forgot she could spot game across state lines if she wanted to. "I didn't know they—"

"Tamika."

"What?" I stood up.

"Cut the shit."

I shrugged. "But I'm—"

"If you knew how much this entire thing has been bothering me you would give me a break by telling me the truth. I deserve that much and you know it."

I looked down.

"I knew it!" She yelled pointing at me.

I sat back down in the seat. "Cut it out."

"What I want to know is why it doesn't bother you." She scooted her chair closer. "I mean you came over here about being put out with no mention about being cheated on."

"Who says it doesn't bother me?" I frowned.

She looked me up and down. "You look like a woman on a mission. Not a woman with a broken heart."

"Nah. I'm just living my best life."

"Tamika, talk to me. Whatever you got planned for them, short of killing anybody, I'd understand."

"Definitely not hurting anyone physically." And I was telling the truth. Before burning down the house the plan was to make sure everyone was out.

She smiled. "Good. So what are you going to do?"

"I can't say."

She grinned. "But it's gonna be good right?"

SILENCE.

"Well?"

"April, I have to go." I stood up and grabbed my purse before kissing her on the cheek.

"Tamika, talk to me." She grabbed my hand. "I know what they doing is all kinds of wrong and you're hurt."

"You have no idea." I was trying to suppress the tears that I told myself I wouldn't allow them to pull from me anymore. But it was hard when I looked into her eyes. Because I knew she sincerely cared about how I felt. To be honest she was the first person to care since all this happened.

"You right. I don't. I mean, I'm a new wife and I can't imagine what I would feel if a relative fucked him."

"Like you did Amina?"

"Ouch."

I sighed. "I'm sorry. That was a low blow."

"And I get it. My only thing I want to tell you is to not let them change you to something worse."

"What if it's too late?"

"Whatever they did to you, you have a right to be mad, just don't let them change you."

"I hear you." I pulled away from her."

"I'm serious."

"I am too, April," I paused. "But it won't happen until I get my revenge." I walked out.

CHAPTER SEVENTEEN

REGGIE

After knocking Amina out and leaving her on the kitchen floor I went to the gym to look for April. I knew her schedule and wanted to talk to her. When I saw her walking up to the gym I pulled up on her. "I gotta talk to you."

"I didn't tell Tamika anything," She said. "She told me."

"What...what?" My jaw hung.

SILENCE.

Slowly she walked over to the passenger side and got in. "Tamika knows," she said.

"Knows...knows what?" It was hard for me to believe.

April stared at me.

"So she really knows about me and—"

"Yes."

"But she couldn't."

"Reggie, I'm telling you that she does."

"I don't, I don't understand how she could and not, not say anything. I mean—"

"Has she done anything strange to you?"

"Nah."

"Are you sure?"

"Yes. I mean, she's been really sweet. It's almost like it was the first time we met and stuff."

"I don't know about all that, Reggie."

"For real. She's patient, kind, sweet and even laid back."

"Is that normal for her?"

I looked ahead at people going into the gym. "I...I..."

"Think clearer, Reggie. Has any one incident happened that caused any kind of problems for you?"

"I'm telling you no!" I yelled. "She hasn't caused any problems and..."

"What?" She asked.

I stared outward harder.

"What is it, Reggie?"

"There ain't been nothing going on with me and Tamika but me and Amina had a situation that was weird not too long ago."

"What was it?"

"Something with a pizza girl."

"I'm confused."

"I took a deep breath and ran my hand down my face. "A pizza girl showed up at the house and I...I..."

"I'm getting bored with you," she said.

I looked at her. "I fucked her."

She sat back and shook her head. "You have issues."

"I do." I admitted.

"Whatever, Reggie."

"I'm serious." I paused. "I have issues and I'm getting help for them too."

"You know what, I like you but not at the expense of my cousins."

"I understand."

"What do you want from me?"

"What you mean?" My thoughts were all over the place. Could Tamika actually have set up the pizza girl incident just to make Amina beef with me harder?

"You asked me to talk for a reason. Now what is it?"

"Oh yeah, you have to be careful."

She frowned. "Why?"

"I think Amina believes we together or something. I have no idea why because I don't talk about you but still."

"Are you kidding me?"

"Like I said I'm not sure but I have a feeling."

"But why?"

"April, if I knew I would tell you where she got the idea."

She scratched her head. "Well, that explains the call."

"When?"

"Some days back. She called my husband and said some nasty things about me. I been trying to get her on the phone for clarification but she keeps hanging up."

"What did she say?"

"Doesn't matter. It all makes sense though like I said."

"It's obvious you don't wanna tell me so I won't press you. Just know that she's dangerous."

She laughed.

"What's funny?" I asked.

"My cousin will never hurt me."

I reached over her leg, opened the glove compartment and pulled out some tissue. Then I pressed it to the back of my head and showed her.

"What is that?" She asked.

"Blood. From the bat she hit me with." I tossed the tissue down. "Now I'm here because she mentioned your name. And if you can't see a problem you in for a rude—"

"Okay," she said cutting me off.

"Okay what?"

"Okay I'll be careful." She sighed. "I still think she hit you because of what you did to her mind but whatever." She waved the air. "Let me get out of here."

CHAPTER EIGHTEEN

AMINA

When Reggie pulled off I quickly pulled up to April before she went into the gym. "April!"

She turned around and walked over to the car and covered her mouth when she saw my face. She walked closer to the driver's side window. "What happened to you?"

"Reggie," I fake cried. "He beat me."

She rushed to the passenger side and got inside. "Why would he do that?"

"I don't know," I said softly. "Maybe because he wanted to kill me since he's afraid of our affair getting out. I mean, with my sister knowing and stuff."

"But...but...I thought you said she wouldn't care."

"I never said that."

"Amina, I thought you—"

"Do you want him or not?" I yelled. I was tired of faking with this bitch.

Silence.

"Answer me!" I said through clenched teeth.

"What is happening to everyone in that house? Since you've been there it's like, it's like everything has gone down hill." She stared at me. "Are you losing your mind?"

"DO...YOU...WANT...MY...MAN...AGAIN?"

She took a deep breath. "No, Amina. Of course not. But you shouldn't want him either."

"I don't believe you."

"You don't have to believe me. What you do have to do is go to the hospital and get somebody to look at your face. And when you're done get somebody to check your heart because—"

STAB! STAB! STAB! STAB! STAB! STAB! STAB! STAB! STAB! STAB! STAB! STAB! STAB! STAB! STAB! STAB! STAB! STAB!

When I was done sticking her eighteen times, I had blood in my hair, mouth and nose. She was doubled over, staring at me with those stupid eyes.

When she finally passed out, I pushed the door open, kicked her out and watched her roll to the ground before I peeled off.

RUSSO

"Thank you, Mrs. Connelly. This is great." I said as my daughter and I finished the spaghetti she warmed up for us.

"Anytime," she smiled. "And any excuse to see you too."

When my daughter dozed off I picked her up and laid her on the sofa. Then I sat back down and took a deep breath.

"What's wrong?" She asked me touching the top of my hand.

"Everything."

"Tell me your worst."

"My wife."

She smiled. "You mean, Amina?"

I nodded and looked at the sofa to be sure my daughter was still sleep. "I know we getting a divorce but..." I took a deep breath again. "I went to drop off Naverly and she wouldn't let me in the house. The house I paid off."

"But you're divorcing her. What makes you think you still have the right?"

"I know all that but..."

"I'm not saying Amina is bad for you because it's not my place. I do know she has a lot of growing up to do like all of you for that matter. And maybe you married way too young to sustain the trials that come with the union."

"But it's her responsibility to take her kid correct?"

"I had a really good friend who lived about a block up the street some years back." She stood up and removed an apple pie from the oven.

"Wait, I met her?"

"No." She sighed and sat the pie on top of the stove. "But when she was younger she had this beautiful little girl." She looked at Naverly. "Almost as pretty as your girl."

I looked at my daughter sleeping and back at her.

"Anyway, she had been out of work for some time." She sat back at the table. "And when her daughter was old enough to tell of things happening to her, she started looking for a job. She felt safe that at the very least her child would be able to speak up for herself and let her know if someone was hurting her."

I sat back and crossed my arms as I listened closely.

"Well, after some time she got an interview for a secretary for this fancy lawyer in downtown DC. She was qualified and if she landed the job it would put her close up to six figures." Mrs. Connelly smiled and looked down before looking at me again. "She was so excited when she told me, Russo. That afterwards, she got to dancing up and down the street and everything. In only her bra and panties mind you."

I laughed. "Whoa."

"I know. But I'm serious too." She paused. "When she got dressed she asked me could I sit with her child but I couldn't that day because of previous church engagements I made." She looked down at her fingers. "That moment still haunts me to this day. And is one of the reasons I never turn you down if you ask."

She looked really sad. "Are you, are you okay?"

"Will be when I get this off my heart. First time I'm even talking about it so let me go through it so it can be done with."

I nodded.

She took a deep breath. "Anyway she asked everyone she could and kept hearing no's. So she decided to ask the child's father."

I moved closer to the table. "Was he in her life?"

"When the mood struck. But mostly no."

I sat back. The dude was nothing like me so I wondered where she was going with it. "And her mother went for him being part time?"

"My friend, like me, believed a child is better suited for the world when it has two parents. She tried things hard in the beginning by dropping her daughter over on him unexpectedly, and even took him to court for child support. But I didn't agree with this brand of parenting."

"I already know how this is gonna go."

"No, son, I don't think you do."

I nodded slowly. "I'm listening."

She took a deep breath. "After consulting with me I convinced her to stop pushing that baby on him. Not that it wasn't his responsibility to help raise her but that he didn't deserve the honor."

She paused. "She took my advice and only released the child to him when he was in the mood and her spirit told her it was safe." She looked into my eyes. "Well this wasn't one of those days."

I clasped my fingers together on the table. This old head definitely knew how to tell a story. "Well what happened?"

"She dropped her child off anyway. This interview was that important but the father of course said he couldn't watch her. Said repeatedly that he wasn't in the mood but she applied pressure and went against everything we talked about." She sighed, got up and cut the pie, before bringing two slices back to the table with silver forks with red handles.

"And?"

"She left the little girl anyway. Came back not even two hours later and the father's door was wide open. His eyes closed tight as he slept on the sofa."

I swallowed the lump in my throat. For some reason I had Naverly's face in my mind and I was already getting heated.

"The daughter was gone. To this day what happened to her remains a mystery. But what is certain is this...they found her face up in the basement of that building. Both legs spread so far apart the limbs were like jelly. The child naked and dead in her own blood."

I sat back. "Why would you tell me a story like that?" I glared.

"You a tough man. That's part of your appeal. But it also means you've seen a lot too." She pointed at me with her fork. "And I know just telling you not to force that child on an unwilling parent wouldn't do the trick. But seeing it..." She took a bite of pie. "Seeing it would change everything."

I shook my head. She was right. That story would fuck me up for life and would probably make things worse even when Naverly grew up. "So what are you saying?"

"I don't know why Amina checked out on being a parent. Could be that she never got over losing her mother and her brother right behind. Guilt can cause you to do the wrong things, to the wrong people if you haven't dealt with the pain."

"Yeah, well I know why she foul." I said thinking of her smashing Reggie.

"Being foul is a symptom of the heart. Something went wrong and she never got it right. It doesn't excuse her for being a bad parent or a bad person. But it does make her, at this moment, unfit to care for your child." She put the fork down and touched my hand. "And that's where you come in."

I sighed. "But I have so much to do with the restaurant and—"

"How is it going?" She smiled. "You know I could always bring over some of my award winning pies."

"I would love that." I sighed. "And it's going good. Still a lot to do though."

"Smart investment of your money. Almost makes how you came about the cash a little easier to swallow."

"Aight, aight."

"I won't say anything else 'bout that," she joked.

"Thanks."

"Did you at least tell your friends about the business?"

"No, not yet," I paused. "Was gonna tell Tamika but...she got some dude who don't want us being cool."

She looked at me funny but didn't say anything out the way. "Well you should let someone know, Russo. Support is always a good thing."

I heard her but there was still the thing about Amina that rubbed me wrong. When my cell rang I picked it up when I saw Tamika's number. When I answered I could barely understand most of what she said. But I did hear this...

April was stabbed! She may be dead!

CHAPTER NINETEEN

TAMIKA

My temples throbbed as I sat in the passenger's side seat of Russo's beamer. He looked over at me and squeezed my hand and I cried harder. "Russo, I'm scared."

"I know, but try not to think the worst," he said as he continued down the road. "April's tough."

I wiped tears away. "Why is this happening? We already lost my mother and brother. Haven't we suffered enough?"

"I don't know why it's happening."

"If she dies—"

"Don't think like that." He looked at the road and then me. "Right now she's fighting and we don't need to make shit worse by thinking the wrong way." He paused. "You talk to your sister?"

I shook my head no.

"Where's Naverly?"

"Mrs. Connelly's watching her."

I sighed. "This is crazy."

"I know. And the police seem clueless."

"The officer told me that the camera couldn't see the assault based on where she was stabbed." I paused. "So basically whoever did it will get away."

"She didn't get raped did she?"

"I don't know, Russo," I cried. "I don't know."

He took a deep breath. "What were you doing at the house? I thought you said Amina threw you out."

I looked at him. "What you mean?"

"I saw the gas can on the side of the house you were holding. You ran out of gas or something?"

I cleared my throat.

I was about to set the house on fire until April's husband told me what happened. So when Russo pulled up I was trying to hide the can but he walked around the back and saw me.

"Ran out of gas," I lied wiping away tears. "That was it."

He nodded. "Let's hope for the best when we get in her room. And try to be calm. I know her husband taking shit heavy."

"My cousin is in the hospital. I can't say what I will do when I get there."

"My bad." He said softly. "Been so busy trying to keep the peace and not fly off the handle that I'm not thinking straight."

"You talking about Amina?" I sniffled.

"Yeah."

"She do something?"

"It's everything to be honest. The fact that I'm letting them fuck and not say nothing like a..." He wiped his hand down his face. "If it wasn't for my daughter."

"I know." I touched his hand. "I know."

He took a deep breath and parked in the lot. We got out and walked into the hospital. When we made it to my cousin's room I broke down when I saw the condition she was in. Russo grabbed me and prevented me from falling. I cried in his arms.

A minute later Reggie came in and rushed toward me before stumbling like his balance was off. "Are you okay?" He asked snatching me from Russo's arms.

I pushed away from him and walked back to Russo.

"She fine," Russo said.

Reggie glared. "Is that right?"

Russo smiled.

Two minutes later Amina came inside and she was beat so bad I thought she was in an accident. I almost didn't recognize her face. Since they came close I figured they came together.

Russo let me go. "What happened to your face?" He asked Amina.

She looked at Reggie and back at Russo. "Got into a fist fight with some girl. I'm fine though."

She walked over to April's bedside and there was something off with my sister. Not only was I pretty sure that Reggie beat her but I was sure of something else.

This feeling sat in my soul.

And gave me chills.

Amina stabbed April.

I knew more than ever that I was gonna burn down that house and make her pay. My sister was dead to me.

BEEEEEEEEP.

When I looked at the machine I saw a line going across the screen.

My cousin was DEAD!

CHAPTER TWENTY

AMINA

April died and I was numb.

I don't know why but when I stabbed her I never thought she would...I mean...die.

KNOCK! KNOCK! KNOCK!

I got off my sofa and walked to the front door. Tamika was on the other side. I took a deep breath and leaned my head on the front door. Did she know I was responsible? Or did she wanna just talk? Either way I wasn't up for it.

"Yes."

"Can you open the door so we can talk?"

"About?"

"April just died yesterday. Can we talk, Amina?" She paused. "Please."

I stood up straight and pulled open the door. Leaning in the doorway I folded my arms across my chest. "What is it?"

"Amina, I wanted to, I wanted to talk to you about Reggie."

I frowned. "What about him?"

"I know."

"What?"

"Everything. That you're sleeping with him."

I laughed. "So you finally opened your eyes and stopped being so naïve. Or did Reggie tell you himself?" I asked, hopeful he finally understood that we were meant to be.

"I knew months ago."

I stood up straight. "Yeah right."

"Amina, I'm telling you I knew."

"So you expect me to believe that you let me and Reggie have sex right under you—"

She threw her hand up. "I knew!"

"So, so, so why did you…"

"Because I had plans. For you both."

"To do what?"

"Destroy what plans you had to be together. But after April died I realized it doesn't matter. All I want is my sister back."

"Tamika, I—"

"Just listen," she paused. "It was so stupid for me to hold on to what I knew but you were wrong too, Amina."

I looked down. "It's not that easy."

"It is that easy. All you—"

"How?"

"How what?" She asked.

"You said you wanted to destroy us right? So how were you planning on doing that?" I glared.

"You don't really wanna know that."

"I'm asking ain't I?"

"The pizza girl. That was me."

My heart thumped. "How, I mean she fucked him in—"

"I hired her."

My eyes widened. Here I thought all this time she was green when...she was...not. "But I got locked up for that bitch."

"You got locked up for fighting over my husband."

"But, I, I still gotta go to court over that!"

"Amina, ma wouldn't want us fighting over anybody. Now lets put everything aside and be family again."

"And Naverly?"

She cleared her throat. "What about her?"

"You know what, Tamika. You came over here to talk so be honest. Do you have anything to do with her being taken away?"

"No."

I didn't believe her. It was in her eyes.

But a part of me missed Tamika. And with April going and getting herself killed by me, I needed someone to talk to since Reggie wasn't available the way I needed.

"Okay, let's put everything bad behind us and start all over," I said.

"Are you serious?"

"Yep," I said nodding my head.

She hugged me and it felt different. Almost like I didn't know her or myself anymore. I mean I knew we shared the same blood but that was all. What was happening to me?

"We have to talk though." I stepped back and let her inside the house. We both sat on the sofa.

"Okay, let's talk," she smiled.

"Are you gonna be able to deal with me and Reggie being together? Because I can't have nobody trying to break us up."

Her jaw dropped.

I put my hand on her shoulder and she looked at my fingers and then my eyes. I moved it away. "Tamika, are you okay?"

"So you still want my husband? Instead of having a sisterhood with me?"

"Wait, so that's your only reason for coming here? To pull me away from my Reggie?" I yelled.

"But you're wrong, Amina!" She said. "Can't you, I mean, I'm confused."

"No, I'm the one who's confused. That man belongs to me and when you said you wanted to repair us I figured you understood that. Now I want a relationship with you but if you—"

"Something is seriously wrong with you, Amina."

I rolled my eyes.

"Amina, you need to get help."

"I don't have to get anything. You're the one who's confused. I am not letting anyone come in the way of Reggie and me. And if we are gonna be sisters you must understand this, Tamika. Because it's not open for discussion. I will be with that man."

SILENCE.

She just stared at me with teary red eyes. Slowly she stood up and walked toward the door. Without saying bye she walked out.

CHAPTER TWENTY-ONE

REGGIE

After April died it was rough. I stayed in a motel because Tamika had yet to call me back and I didn't want to go back to that house without her. I made a decision not to stay in the house because I had to get my shit together.

I refused to have sex with anything out here and I refused to deal with Amina. I don't know what was on her mind but for me I was good and didn't want her in my life.

Right before I went into Russo's condo building my phone rang. I walked away from the door and answered when I saw it was my wife. "Hello, you, hi, I mean—"

"What do you want, Reggie?"

"Tamika, I know you mad at me and—"

"Hurt."

"I know you're hurt but you have to understand what me and Amina did means nothing."

"That's not what she thinks."

"I don't give a fuck what she thinks! And I know this is all...I know it's crazy but—"

"You ruined my sister's life. And you ruined mine. I'm done with you, Reggie. For good."

It sounded like she hung up.

"TAMIKA! TAMIKA! TAMIKA!" I paused. "Are you there?"

"Yes."

I took a deep breath and leaned against his building. "Don't, please don't do this now." I paused. "Let's meet in person first. Okay?"

Silence.

"Tamika, please. I know it's wrong for me to ask anything of you but I'm a sick man and I'm getting help. And I don't want anything from you but time. No commitment." I paused and waited to hear her voice. "Please, baby."

It seemed like forever and then...

"Okay." She said.

I could breathe.

"Thank you...so much." I paused. "When can we meet?"

"I'll call you."

CLICK.

"Tamika?" I looked at the phone.

She hung up.

RUSSO

When I opened the door Reggie was standing in front of me. My jaw twitched as I looked at him. The rage had me wanting to zap out on this nigga.

"Can I come in, man?"

I stepped back and let him inside. He followed me to the kitchen. I sat at the table and crossed my arms over my chest. He took a seat across from me.

"Let me stop you," I said.

"Okay."

"I know you fucking my wife. And been fucking her. What I want to know is why?"

He wiped his hand down his face. "How'd you know?"

"Like I said, been knowing for months."

Reggie sat down and leaned back. "So you just let—"

"Allowed. I allowed you to fuck her."

"I'm confused."

"I allowed you and that slut to do what you wanted because I was over her. And for the sake of my daughter I wanted to keep the peace. But trust me when I say there's a time limit on your union."

He frowned. "Look, man, I'm sorry but—"

"Are you? Because to Tamika and me it looks like yah niggas been disrespecting for months without giving any fucks. And pushing it in our faces too. Luckily for you I fell out of love wit' that bitch when she went psycho on me but I'm not giving forever passes."

"I'ma need you to stop threatening me, Russo."

"Or what? Exactly what the fuck you gonna do if I don't?" I asked him.

He took a deep breath like I gave a fuck. "Russo, I was wrong. And I know you not trying to hear it but it's true."

"Quite honestly, I'm not trying to hear none of this shit. And I suggest you make the next fourteen years of your life the best because I know what I'ma do."

"You know what, I'm sick of this shit." He stole me in the face. It was so quick I almost didn't see him coming. But it was sneaky enough to knock me out my chair.

I got up as fast as I could but I was never one hundred percent after being paralyzed but I could move some. Once on my feet I grabbed him by his collar with my left hand and stole him in the jaw with my right.

He kneed me and I doubled over, holding my stomach. He used the time to hit me in the back of my head with a pan I had on the stove. When I was on the floor he hit me several times more and then...

CHAPTER TWENTY-TWO

TAMIKA

"You don't know him like I do," Reggie and me were in my motel room, standing by the door because I didn't want him getting comfortable. He was telling me about the fight he had with Russo like he was surprised. "We like brothers. Why would he come at me like this?"

I glared at him. He and my sister were two parts crazy. "That's before you fucked his wife." I paused. "And what do you want with me exactly?"

"I came here to say I thought about our situation. I think we should leave everything and everybody and start a new life."

"I'm not doing that."

"Why?"

"Because you fucked up my life. You made mistakes and what I'm going to do now is focus on me."

"But I can't let you go."

"You don't have a choice if it's what I want."

He moved closer and touched my elbow. "But I want you."

"Even if I considered it, which I'm not, my sister has already said she's not letting you go. And I'm not gonna spend a life worrying about you and her being together." I thought about the gas container on the side of the house. "I won't have to."

"What does that mean?"

Silence.

"Tamika, what does that mean?"

"Just leave me alone."

He took a deep breath. "I'm going to the gym. Please don't make a permanent decision on us. Not yet."

"You been to the gym a lot lately."

"I'm changing up how I deal with stress. The gym is perfect."

I rolled my eyes.

He grabbed my hand softly. "I'm serious. And I know you don't believe me but there is a lot I want to tell you about. Things about my past."

"Like what?"

"Things that involved my mother. She was murdered a few weeks back."

My eyes widened and the tenseness I had in my arms went away. "Oh my, god, Reggie. I'm sorry."

"Tamika, don't worry about it. Like I said I'm not trying to gain pity by telling you. I'm not trying to gain anything. I just want you to know that a lot has been put into perspective and I will repair our bond."

He kissed me on the cheek and walked out.

I sat on the bed with my jaw hung. I didn't like his mother but I didn't want her dead either. I was still thinking about her when my phone rang.

"Hello," I said without looking at the number.

"Hey, Mika."

"Russo." I laid back on the bed.

"You 'aight?" He asked.

"Uh, yeah, why?"

"Your voice sounds out of it."

"Oh, yeah," I sighed. "Reggie just told me his mother died."

"For real?" He asked with passion.

"Yeah," I paused. "It's crazy."

"Where is he?" He said in a sincere tone.

"At the gym probably. He always goes there when he's stressed."

"Damn, I'm sorry to hear about his moms. She wasn't for me but I wouldn't wish ill will on her you know?"

"I feel the same way." I took a deep breath and rolled over on the bed. "I heard about the fight though."

"I ain't worried about that. We brothers and we gonna be good. Always."

"He said the same thing." I was surprised to hear Russo was taking it so well. Maybe Mrs. Connelly's words did work on him. "That's good to hear."

"But look, I gotta go. I'll get up with you later."

RUSSO

I hung up the phone with Tamika. "He at the gym." I said to my men, Craig, Jackson and Paul.

"What you want us to do again?" Paul asked me.

The three of them were brothers. Craig was the oldest at forty-six, Jackson was thirty and Paul was in his twenties. Now I liked using them for murder when I was deeper in the streets but Paul was always and idiot. I'd have to spend three times explaining myself to him and it irritated me.

I had to pick up my daughter from Mrs. Connelly and I wanted Reggie's death swift and immediate.

"Listen, talk to your brothers about the details," I said to Paul before giving them the address. "But get it done."

"We got you," Craig said. "Let's go."

I watched him and his brothers walk out and sat down. I looked at Reggie like a brother but after what he did to me in my kitchen, and this shit with my wife I was done.

It was time for revenge.

THE THREE BROTHERS

Having worked with Reggie before, the brothers parked in a black van and sat in the parking lot of the gym. After two hours Reggie walked out and without wasting time Paul threw open the back doors and started shooting in his direction.

Seeing the assassination in action, Reggie dropped to the ground as people ran everywhere. Some back inside the gym and others to their cars.

The other brothers, seeing the melee and realizing that Paul moved too quickly, pulled off to get away. Since the door was open Paul fell to the ground, with the assault rifle in his hand.

Terrified of getting caught, he dropped the gun and ran into a nearby office building. Opening a janitor's closet, he walked inside and sat on the floor. Sweaty and out of breath he waited.

Within minutes the sirens grew so loud it was as if they were outside the door. His breath quickened as he heard many footsteps rushing towards him. The door flew open and barrels, belonging to the policemen aimed in his direction.

"Russo!" Paul blurted out. "His name is Russo!"

AMINA

I was sitting on the sofa texting Reggie. I hit him multiple times with no answer. I figured I would give him some time to cool off.

When the front door opened Reggie walked inside. He looked out of breath and scared. He closed and locked the door and looked out all of the windows before walking over to me.

"What's wrong?" I asked him.

"I think, I think Russo tried to have me killed."

My jaw dropped. "What? But, why?"

"Because of you and me and everything else I guess." He plopped on the sofa. And even though he was on edge I was happy to have him around me.

"I'm glad you're here because I meant to tell you that I forgive you for hitting me."

"Well I don't forgive you. And, Amina, we done. I'm sorry for letting my need to have sex compromise everything but even if I don't make it with my wife you and me won't be together again. Ever."

"You don't mean that."

I looked down at myself, trying to understand why he would say that. And then it all made sense. "Oh wow, look at me. I'm a mess. Let me go clean up and—"

"Amina, it won't matter."

"Please," I grabbed his hand. "Let me get myself together. Maybe put on some makeup to cover some of these bruises."

"Whatever, Amina."

I smiled and jumped up. "And Reggie, I know you don't want to hear this but being with you for this short period of time has been the best of me. And you might not feel the same but I wanted you to know." I smiled and ran upstairs to run the water in the tub.

I added banana scented bath oil because I wanted to smell sweet for him. When I did this in the past he said I was good enough to eat. After I slid in the tub I knew things would change. I hoped they would change for the better but I couldn't be sure.

Thinking about everything, as I sat in the tub, I don't know why I gravitated toward Reggie. All I know is that I feel the way I feel and want what I want. And as far as my sister is concerned I guess we'll see.

Wait...I smell something burning.

What...what is that?

EPILOGUE

ONE WEEK LATER

*T*amika sat in the front row at April's funeral alone. No one on the left or right to support her. The family had been torn apart over the last few months and it took everything in her not to use drugs but she was determined to stay strong and she succeeded.

After hugging April's husband, she walked outside only to see Reggie leaning against a car she didn't recognize across the street from the church. She was shocked because she hadn't seen or heard from him in days.

She walked toward him.

"How are you?" He asked standing up straight.

"What are you doing here?"

"I'm sorry, because I know you haven't heard from me, but I had to get away with Russo thinking I put the police on to him. And the hit he got on my head. Things been rough."

She sighed. "My sister's dead and you coming at me about things being rough for you?"

"That's what I wanted to talk to you about," he paused. "I had nothing to do with burning down the house, Tamika. I mean I wanted her to leave me alone but not like this."

Tamika looked up the street and back at him. "You not the only one people suspect. They saying it could be me because of your affair and Russo because of the affair too. Right now the police are still investigating but things are getting bad."

He took a deep breath and looked away. "You heard from him?"

"Russo? Even if I did I wanna keep my relationship with Russo separate. With this war *that you have going on...I mean...it's better this way."*

"You cool with him even after the nigga tried to kill me?" He glared.

"Reggie, Amina is gone. She had problems but I still loved her. Add to that someone murdering my cousin and I just can't be heavy with you right now. I'm sorry."

He nodded and looked around. "I'm sorry. Just want to try and work on us since no one can stop us from being together now." He paused. "But look, this is my new number." He handed her a sheet of paper. "Call me when you can, so we can talk." He kissed her on the cheek, got in his car and rolled away.

When Reggie left Tamika walked up the street and waited for Russo. When he pulled up she looked around and slid in his car. After all the melee at the gym the police wanted Russo so he

was trying to keep a low profile.

As they drove down the street there were still a

lot of people wanting to know, who killed Amina

Jameson?

CARTEL PUBLICATIONS
PRESENTS

The Cartel Publications Order Form

www.thecartelpublications.com

Inmates **ONLY** receive novels for $10.00 per book **PLUS** shipping fee **PER BOOK.**

(Mail Order **MUST** come from inmate directly to receive discount)

Shyt List 1	_____	$15.00
Shyt List 2	_____	$15.00
Shyt List 3	_____	$15.00
Shyt List 4	_____	$15.00
Shyt List 5	_____	$15.00
Pitbulls In A Skirt	_____	$15.00
Pitbulls In A Skirt 2	_____	$15.00
Pitbulls In A Skirt 3	_____	$15.00
Pitbulls In A Skirt 4	_____	$15.00
Pitbulls In A Skirt 5	_____	$15.00
Victoria's Secret	_____	$15.00
Poison 1	_____	$15.00
Poison 2	_____	$15.00
Hell Razor Honeys	_____	$15.00
Hell Razor Honeys 2	_____	$15.00
A Hustler's Son	_____	$15.00
A Hustler's Son 2	_____	$15.00
Black and Ugly	_____	$15.00
Black and Ugly As Ever	_____	$15.00
Ms Wayne & The Queens of DC **(LGBT)**	_____	$15.00
Black And The Ugliest	_____	$15.00
Year Of The Crackmom	_____	$15.00
Deadheads	_____	$15.00
The Face That Launched A Thousand Bullets	_____	$15.00
The Unusual Suspects	_____	$15.00
Paid In Blood	_____	$15.00
Raunchy	_____	$15.00
Raunchy 2	_____	$15.00
Raunchy 3	_____	$15.00
Mad Maxxx (4th Book Raunchy Series)	_____	$15.00
Quita's Dayscare Center	_____	$15.00
Quita's Dayscare Center 2	_____	$15.00
Pretty Kings	_____	$15.00
Pretty Kings 2	_____	$15.00
Pretty Kings 3	_____	$15.00
Pretty Kings 4	_____	$15.00
Silence Of The Nine	_____	$15.00
Silence Of The Nine 2	_____	$15.00
Silence Of The Nine 3	_____	$15.00
Prison Throne	_____	$15.00
Drunk & Hot Girls	_____	$15.00
Hersband Material **(LGBT)**	_____	$15.00
The End: How To Write A Bestselling Novel In 30 Days (Non-Fiction Guide)	_____	$15.00
Upscale Kittens	_____	$15.00
Wake & Bake Boys	_____	$15.00
Young & Dumb	_____	$15.00
Young & Dumb 2: Vyce's Getback	_____	$15.00

By KIM MEDINA

215

Tranny 911 **(LGBT)**	_____	$15.00
Tranny 911: Dixie's Rise **(LGBT)**	_____	$15.00
First Comes Love, Then Comes Murder	_____	$15.00
Luxury Tax	_____	$15.00
The Lying King	_____	$15.00
Crazy Kind Of Love	_____	$15.00
Goon	_____	$15.00
And They Call Me God	_____	$15.00
The Ungrateful Bastards	_____	$15.00
Lipstick Dom **(LGBT)**	_____	$15.00
A School of Dolls **(LGBT)**	_____	$15.00
Hoetic Justice	_____	$15.00
KALI: Raunchy Relived	_____	$15.00
(5th Book in Raunchy Series)		
Skeezers	_____	$15.00
Skeezers 2	_____	$15.00
You Kissed Me, Now I Own You	_____	$15.00
Nefarious	_____	$15.00
Redbone 3: The Rise of The Fold	_____	$15.00
The Fold (4th Redbone Book)	_____	$15.00
Clown Niggas	_____	$15.00
The One You Shouldn't Trust	_____	$15.00
The WHORE The Wind		
Blew My Way	_____	$15.00
She Brings The Worst Kind	_____	$15.00
The House That Crack Built	_____	$15.00
The House That Crack Built 2	_____	$15.00
The House That Crack Built 3	_____	$15.00
The House That Crack Built 4	_____	$15.00
Level Up **(LGBT)**	_____	$15.00
Villains: It's Savage Season	_____	$15.00
Gay For My Bae	_____	$15.00

(**Redbone 1 & 2** are **NOT** Cartel Publications novels and if **ordered** the cost is **FULL** price of $15.00 **each. No Exceptions.**)

Please add $5.00 **PER BOOK** for shipping and handling. **Inmates** too!

The Cartel Publications * P.O. BOX 486 OWINGS MILLS MD 21117

Name: _____

Address: _____

City/State: _____

Contact/Email: _____

Please allow 7-10 BUSINESS days before shipping.
The Cartel Publications is NOT responsible for Prison Orders rejected!

NO RETURNS and NO REFUNDS.
NO PERSONAL CHECKS ACCEPTED
STAMPS NO LONGER ACCEPTED